UNLOCKING DARKNESS

Keys to Love, Book Five

Kennedy Layne

UNLOCKING DARKNESS

Dedication

Jeffrey—Another series complete with so many more to go! Thank you for being my partner on this crazy writing journey. I love you!

Cole—You're completing a series of your own...your first semester of college. We are so proud of you!

CHAPTER ONE

Twelve years ago…

WHEN DID A person accept their fate?

Emma Irwin's hope for being saved had all but been extinguished. No one was going to save her from the hands of this monster. No one even knew she was on a boat in the middle of the lake with someone she'd mistakenly trusted her entire life. He'd been a close family friend, a helpful neighbor, and someone she would have never thought could be so intimately cruel.

"I'll come and visit with you."

Emma swallowed against the bile that rose in her throat. She lifted her face toward the darkened sky that was crying the tears she couldn't. She'd literally gone completely numb, but she wasn't sure that was due to the cold or the fact that he was taking her to her death.

She wasn't ready to die so young.

The fishing boat rocked back and forth as the waves churned fiercely. The gusts of wind were following the storm to the east, though the rumbling of thunder could still be heard over the steady hum of the engine. There were no stars to be seen, no moon to light the way…only angry streaks of lightning that signaled the end was near.

Would she be dead long before the storm had passed?

Emma was no longer shivering as her thoughts once again

turned to her family. She didn't want them to think she wasn't happy. Would they believe that she no longer loved them? How was it possible to miss them so much while she was still breathing?

She would give absolutely anything to be back home, warm and comfortable in her bed. As it stood, tomorrow morning would dawn a new day filled with people moving to and from without her anywhere to be found.

That longing for what she would probably never experience again gave her one last ounce of strength to fight against the smiling monster that had been hidden amongst the residents of Blyth Lake.

Emma kicked her legs with as much force as she could muster, trying desperately to grab the side of the boat. Her reaction did seem to stun him, but only for a second. He grabbed her wet strands of hair and all but threw her against one of the vinyl-covered cushions that were mounted to the square bench seats that spanned the width of the fishing boat. With her wrists bound behind her back, it had been a futile attempt. She landed once again on the aluminum bottom of the boat, causing her to cry out in pain when her hands dug into her lower back.

"Why are you fighting this?" He began wrapping her legs tightly in a metal chain that never seemed to end. She wasn't sure why she continued to scream when no one was around to hear her pleas. By this point, she barely had a voice left. "I'll bring you a sister soon, I promise. Until then, I'll come and visit with you as much as possible. We will all be a family…the one I've always wanted."

Emma tried to tell him that she already had a family—a mother and father who loved her very much. She also had a sister who she worshiped, not that Shae would ever know that to be the truth. Their last words had been said in anger, and nothing Emma did now could take back those words of animosity said only in the heat of the moment.

Tears that she didn't know she could still cry slid out of the corners of her eyes and mingled with the rain coming down from the black sky above.

This was it.

This was the end.

"Please don't do this. Please. Please. I don't want to die. I—"

He kissed her gently on the forehead, ignoring her pleas as he gathered her in his arms. She writhed and did her best to make this hard for him, but she was wasting her last few seconds struggling against his overwhelming strength.

"Don't! Don't do this. You don't have to—"

The cold water swallowed her whole.

She didn't even have a chance to take a breath before the water closed around her, almost as if to welcome her with open arms. It was instinctive to fight against the suction dragging her down into the depths. She struggled, not caring that she was tearing the flesh right off her wrists.

She continued to sink lower and lower against her will. The temperature changed faster and faster as she sank to the bottom.

Her chest began to burn for oxygen and her ears filled with a pressure that was almost unbearable. She fought against the darkness and the cold, but it was now all around her. She held out hope, just like her father would have wanted her to do, anticipating for someone to save her.

Emma waited and waited for someone to grab her from above and pull her from this nightmare, but help never came. She had no choice but to part her lips and draw in the darkness.

CHAPTER TWO

Present day...

"WHAT DO YOU mean he's running around the Foster's field naked?"

"He's trying to signal the aliens," Deputy Byron replied as if this was a normal conversation. The only thing that gave him away was the slight lift to the corner of his mouth. "The fifth of whiskey probably didn't help matters."

Mitch Kendall closed his eyes and rubbed his forehead in frustration, but nothing was going to ease the throbbing that had pretty much set up permanent residence since his return home. He'd actually found himself debating if another deployment to Afghanistan with his former unit wouldn't have been a better alternative than dealing with the local crazies in his hometown of Blyth Lake, Ohio.

Having a sadistic serial killer in their midst for over a decade certainly didn't help matters.

"Naked. You know, devoid of any clothing?" Byron reiterated, grabbing the keys to the deputies' vehicle. He didn't immediately head to the door. "Aren't you going to drive out there with me, Sheriff?"

Mitch heard a discreet cough that had to have come from Patty, who was sitting in her usual spot behind the front desk of the small police station. The dispatcher had been doing this job since before he'd left for boot camp sixteen years ago. She didn't blink an eye at such absurd calls, but she'd also grown up around these parts.

"I understand that Sheriff Percy would have accompanied you, but we're talking about Shelby Tilmadge. He's harmless as an old tick hound and just like his father. All he wants is some attention." Mitch waited for Byron to take the cue he'd been given and leave. It appeared that a little bit of incentive was needed. "After you get Shelby wrapped up…well, clothed and back to his residence, at the very least…go on home yourself. Feel free to take your cruiser instead of coming back to the station for your personal vehicle. That's your part of town. Showing some police presence isn't such a bad idea, anyway."

"I appreciate that. I have dinner plans tonight."

Mitch would have gladly asked Byron who the lucky girl was if it had been any other day, but that wasn't going to happen this evening. Technically, it was only a little after sixteen hundred hours—four o'clock for civilian folks. He was running on maybe two hours of sleep after spending most of that time in the woods searching for the individual who'd all but waged war on his family and terrorized the town.

"Have a good night, Byron." Mitch headed back to his office, but he stopped short of the doorway when he saw the team of feds wrapping up for the day. Shit. There was still one more thing he needed to do before he called it a night himself. "Thorne, any updates from your end?"

"No." Special Agent Jay Thorne closed the file that had been laying open on the table he and his team had confiscated as a larger workspace than the average-sized desks the station offered. "The only thing we have going for us is that your sister grazed the unsub when she fired a round in an attempt to stop him from attacking her. We removed the slug from the doorframe and sent it off to the lab in hopes of collecting some trace evidence, but we're talking close to two weeks before we receive any results."

"Even then, the perp would need to be in the system for us to get a hit on a viable DNA sample," Mitch said resignedly.

He'd been military most of his life until recently, but that didn't mean he wasn't aware of how things worked in the civilian world. The federal government used the same process to examine evidence as the military's Defense Intelligence Service did in tracking high-valued targets.

A dull ache began to form in his hip, a memory of those times and places where he'd belonged to the action arm of ferreting out the truly evil people from inhabiting the far-flung reaches of this wide world. His body was now letting him know that he'd been on his feet for too long. His age and experience were catching up with him.

"Are you guys heading out for the night?" Mitch asked, knowing he wouldn't be so lucky. He had quite a few items to clear up on his desk.

"We're all running on fumes." Thorne gestured for the three other men to go ahead of him. "I've submitted the daily report and the after action on last night's goat rope to one of our profiling teams. I've included an updated summary of the details that we ran to ground, and I'm hoping to get a current profile of the unsub back in a few days."

Mitch debated reminding the federal agent that he'd said virtually the same thing last week, but it no longer mattered. A chip had been called in that couldn't be taken back. Thorne wasn't going to like it, but this was still Mitch's town. He was ultimately responsible to the townsfolk who he served to protect.

"About that," Mitch began, only to come up short when there was no polite way to verbalize that Thorne's routine chain of command OODA Loop was too fucking slow for the current situation. "You should know that I called in a favor from an old friend currently working out of Quantico. Special Agent Allison Delaney is arriving in Blyth Lake tomorrow."

"Like hell she is," Thorne exclaimed in anger, leaning forward and resting his fists on the table in front of him. His reaction was expected. "Sheriff, you can't just ring up some old war buddy over in D.C. and have them twist Quantico's tail to request your own personal profiler. It doesn't work like that. Special Agent Theo Stringer is damned good at his job, but you need to understand that he has to prioritize his cases. The Bureau—"

Thorne immediately recognized his mistake, and Mitch didn't bother to smooth it over for him. Instead, he mimicked Thorne's posture and rested his knuckles on the opposite side of the table. He didn't give a shit what level of authority Thorne held in the Bureau.

Mitch understood without a shadow of a doubt that he held the ace. Besides, he had more field experience in his right thumb than this little noob, and there wasn't a chance in hell he was dealing with bureaucracy when it came to his family.

"My sister was attacked in her own home last night by a sadistic fuck who has murdered over eighteen women spanning over twelve years that we're currently aware of. Gwen received twenty-six stitches to close a wound that was sliced open by a knife that could very easily have been used to kill her had this son of a bitch ever gotten the upper hand."

Mitch was usually more adept at handling these types of situations, and Thorne really wasn't a bad guy to deal with. He was actually a hell of an agent, but this was just another case in what would be a long line of investigations to him. It wasn't daily fare for Mitch, though.

This case had become personal.

"Special Agent Delaney won't be here in a professional capacity for the FBI. She took two weeks' leave to come visit an old friend. If it gets back to your boss as anything other than two friends reconnecting, I *will* use my considerable contacts outside of your division to have any future you might have rat-holed in some backwater shithole somewhere outside of Tucumcari, New Mexico. Your ass will be shuffling papers for the remainder of your goddamned career. Do we understand each other?"

Thorne's jawline became taut in his irritation, and Mitch braced himself for what he suspected would be a halfhearted rebuttal at best. In all fairness, he wouldn't have blamed the man had he drawn a line. He sure as hell didn't have to let Mitch in on any part of this investigation, seeing as the murders now fell under federal jurisdiction.

Thorne was here to do a job. Any interference Mitch or the sheriff's department introduced into the investigation would fall on his shoulders.

"I'm going to let this conversation slide, Kendall, because of what happened last night. I understand more than you know." The fact that Thorne didn't refer to Mitch as sheriff was telling, but he didn't care as long as Thorne understood where the line was drawn from here on out. There were quite a few favors that were owed to him, and he didn't mind collecting. Hell, it was the sole reason he'd ignored his pride and requested that Allie take some personal leave to help with the investigation…off the books, of course. "Look, I'd be the same way if I were in your shoes. This unsub has dragged your family into this mess repeatedly, and we've been damned fortunate that we haven't lost anyone else."

Thorne finally sighed in resignation as he straightened his shoulders and rubbed his eyes in exhaustion. It had been a very long thirty-six hours for all of them. Mitch's announcement certainly hadn't ended the evening on a good note.

"Just promise me that Special Agent Delaney won't hinder this investigation in any way. When we catch this son of a bitch, I don't want a judge to let him go on a damned technicality."

Mitch nodded his agreement to the first part of that statement, but he wasn't so sure there was a need to stress over the latter. He honestly didn't think this sick and twisted individual wanted to be taken alive. Even if he had, Mitch wasn't sure he'd allow him that opportunity.

"You have my word."

Thorne tapped the table in approval before heading toward the front, stopping long enough to say goodnight to Patty. Mitch began to walk to his private office in the back, but he stopped at the threshold when Thorne called out his name.

"I don't want Delaney in this office. And for the record, that's non-negotiable."

Mitch could live with that stipulation, so once again he nodded his agreement. It was better than the alternative, which Thorne could have easily employed.

Mitch was personally acquainted with a few officers who had taken command positions, both at the Pentagon and at various other agencies around Washington. In particular, he had one or two contacts with the NRO, and those men and women were in positions to literally move mountains.

He didn't for one second believe that his hands were tied. It was just a damned good thing that the military had taught him how to improvise in certain situations and to apply the minimum amount of pressure required to affect the change he needed.

"Patty, go on home," Mitch instructed kindly, knowing full well that she'd been into the station earlier than normal after last night's events. "Let Special Agent Thorne walk you out to your car. It's the least he can do."

It was still light outside, but taking precautions weren't a bad idea at a time like this.

Thorne lifted the side of his mouth in response, but he was too much of a gentleman to ignore the request. The majority of those federal boys were a bunch of Ivy League Boy Scouts. Too many of them were throttled by a suffocating bureaucracy to take the risks that were often required to bring a case like this one to an appropriate end.

This son of a bitch needed to die...not stand trial for a year making headlines.

Mitch recognized that he was being harsh on the federal agents who had come to town to do a job. They were good men with good intentions. He blamed his current mood on the fact that he had to go another night without closure on this case.

He took the time to revel in the quietness that shortly followed after Thorne and Patty left the station. He walked into his private office, ignoring the boxes that he'd yet to unpack. Besides, it was only his way of denying the fact that he'd most likely end up taking the sheriff's position permanently come election time.

The low chime of the door buzzer signaled someone had entered the station. Mitch hadn't even had time to roll his chair up to his desk when his father made an appearance at his door.

"Dad, everything alright?"

Gus Kendall didn't reply right away, but instead slowly made his way to one of the two guest chairs that were positioned in front of Mitch's desk. His father sank into what had to be the most uncomfortable seat in the station, removing the toothpick from his mouth. The strain around his blue eyes was noticeable.

"We almost lost your sister last night."

"We didn't lose her," Mitch corrected, hoping that his statement hit home. Their father had been through hell these past three years after losing his one and only wife. He shouldn't have to think there was a chance he could outlive one of his children. "Gwen fought back and took away his initiative. Special Agent Thorne has a detail sitting outside of her farmhouse as we speak."

"A lot of good that will do," Gus irately replied with good reason. He pointed the toothpick Mitch's way to emphasis his words. "The original protection detail never should have been pulled from her to begin with, and you know it. When Detective Kendrick handed everything over to the feds, this case should have been finished up within days."

"It doesn't work like it does on TV, Dad." Mitch understood everyone's frustration, but each decision in this case had been weighed to the fullest. Thorne had done what he felt was in the best interest of the investigation and also within the budget he was allowed. "Agent Thorne and his team are doing the best they can, given the evidence and the circumstances."

The dull ache that had made itself known was now raging war inside Mitch's head. He couldn't believe he'd been reduced to defending the feds when he'd gone behind their back himself only hours ago to bring in someone he trusted.

"I asked Gwen if she'd come back to stay at the house for a little while," Gus revealed, looking down at his toothpick. Mitch had only ever seen this sense of helplessness on the man once before, and that was when Mary Kendall had been on her deathbed. "You know, at least until she's healed."

"That's not what you meant, and she probably knows that." Mitch stood from his chair that he'd never rolled closer to his workspace. He walked around the desk and took the other guest chair so that he could be closer to his father. "Dad, Gwen is going to be fine. Chad will be staying with her for the time being, and you know for a fact that the Noah, Jace, and Lance will be hovering over her until we get this son of a bitch behind bars or into the morgue."

"It's good to have you boys back to look after things," Gus said softly, the black and white clock on the wall ticking louder than his voice. "It's good to have all of you home."

Mitch leaned back in the chair and quietly sat with his dad, knowing that's all that needed to be said. Gus Kendall didn't want to return home to an empty house. No one would, under the circumstances. All he'd do was sit and worry about his children, as would any parent.

Mitch and his siblings had returned to Blyth Lake after they'd all served their country. It was a family tradition, and one that they'd proudly carried on over the years. He and his three brothers had served in the Marines, while Gwen had joined the Navy. It had been his intention to serve the full twenty years, but a few pieces of shrapnel had somewhat altered that plan.

He'd been the first to recognize when he'd been unable to physically continue doing what was needed to do on a daily basis. He'd refused to drag it out to retirement and debase himself in doing so.

Sixteen years served honorably and faithfully was listed on the papers, but he'd been given an early retirement on a medical basis. He couldn't argue with that, especially seeing as he was still walking and able to do for himself. A few pins and rods made of metal helped with that, but it was better than returning home like so many of his own heroes had.

"How's the house working out?" Gus asked, most likely getting annoyed at the clock above the desk. "Did you ever get someone to fix the fence around the east field?"

"Not yet," Mitch replied, not going into further detail. This murder case had been eating away practically every minute of the day, but he didn't want to remind his father of that. Hell, Mitch was lucky he even had time to take a piss. "I'd actually like to do some of the fence work myself. I should have time yet before the first snowfall."

To say that he and his siblings had been surprised to all be given keys to homesteads on their return home was an understatement. Granted, none of the houses were *brand* new. They were established properties that needed quite a bit of renovations, but that's the way the Kendall family did things. They worked for what they had, and they were proud of doing things that way.

Mary Kendall had received a sizable inheritance from her father, though she'd never spent a dime of it on herself. She and Gus had squirreled it away for a very special occasion, though it remained unspoken that a bit of pride may have come into the picture.

Gus Kendall had worked with his hands his entire life, and his own business of crafting handmade high-quality wooden furniture had put food on the table and clothes on their children's backs. He'd provided for his family the only way he knew how, and that was important around these parts.

In the end, it had been their mother's dying wish that those properties in their childhood hometown be purchased for her children to raise their own families in someday. And here they all were—back home.

"We'll catch this son of a bitch, Dad," Mitch promised quietly, having already explained to his family that he'd called in a favor from an old friend. He'd spoken to Allie earlier this afternoon, so he wasn't expecting her to arrive until tomorrow. "In the meantime, we're doing the best we can to protect the residents of Blyth Lake."

"Everyone is on edge," Gus admitted with a slight shake of

his head. "Harlan Whitmore, Chester Mayer, Calvin Arlos, and even Tiny Phifer are talking about creating some type of neighborhood watch for the town as a whole. Hell, even Jeremy Bell said he'd help out and walk a patrol. With his health issues, he's lucky he can cross the street without passing out."

"Jeremy Bell was the last to lose his daughter," Mitch gently reminded his father, knowing it was hitting a little too close to home. "He wants this lunatic caught even more than the rest of us."

"I came very close to being in Jeremy's shoes last night." Gus compressed his lips together as he ruminated over the danger his family had been placed in since their return. "I'm beginning to think—"

"Don't you dare say it, Dad." Mitch rested his elbows on his knees as he leaned forward to make sure his point got across. "It was time for all of us to come home. None of us regret returning to Blyth Lake, not even Gwen."

"A homecoming is supposed to be a time of rejoicing, son. It just feels as if we're all fighting for our lives here."

Mitch understood why his dad would have that sentiment at the moment.

Yes, young girls from the community and beyond had been abducted and killed, only to end up at the bottom of the lake in their own little makeshift graveyard. But it wasn't just their lives that had been ruined. Mitch could only hope that those victims found peace in death, while those left behind had to deal with the pain of that loss until they took their own dying breaths.

"We *are* fighting for our lives, Dad," Mitch agreed, tacking on something that he believed they should all take to heart. "We're fighting against a darkness that descended on this town a long time ago, and it's time to reclaim what's rightfully ours."

CHAPTER THREE

"**G**OOD MORNING, YOUNG lady."

Allie Delaney looked over her shoulder, but no one was there. She realized that the older gentleman rearranging the cornstalks outside the hardware store was actually talking to her. He was the second individual to do so without having any idea of who she was. It was rather endearing to have complete strangers speak to her this early in the morning as a courtesy with no alternative agenda.

"Good morning, sir," Allie replied with a smile. Her mood continued to brighten in spite of the severe lack of caffeine she'd had since leaving Virginia at such a godforsaken hour that it dare not be repeated, and that was saying something, considering her background. "I like your decorations."

To say that Blyth Lake was a quaint town practically snatched from a canvas of a Norman Rockwell painting was a bit of an understatement. She'd thought these kinds of places had been phased out and been replaced with suburban strip malls for as far as the eye could see. When she'd driven past the blue and white population sign, there had been tended flower beds with the most beautiful blooms she'd ever seen—and it was nearly the end of October.

Who was lucky enough to have a green thumb, along with the time to nurse along flowers growing in a public easement? The people here in this small town had something very special going for them. They also had something equally as bad against them, which was the very reason she was here in the first place.

"We're hosting an early trick or treating event tomorrow night for the kids and their parents. All the shops are joining in to make it as much of a success as we can manage." The older gentleman continued to talk, so Allie slowed her pace until she'd come to a complete stop nearby. "Did you get settled into the B&B okay? I'm surprised you're out and about this early after coming in on the redeye."

Allie had to have misunderstood what the man said. That wouldn't be a hard feat, considering the exhaustion she was battling.

She attempted to maintain her casual outward appearance while she tried to figure out how it was possible for him to know where she was staying, as well as the fact that she'd taken a redeye out of D.C. Not even Mitch Kendall, the man she'd flown out to see, had known of her travel schedule.

So much for this place being too good to be true.

"I'm sorry, but I didn't catch your name," Allie said nonchalantly, steering the conversation back toward him.

Allie would take this man's name and run him through the NCIS database the first chance she got. It was clear he was delighted with himself that he'd caught her off guard. He didn't fit the profile of the serial killer that she'd been personally requested to flesh out, but that didn't mean he didn't have some association with the unsub or a partnership of some sort.

It certainly wasn't unheard of in past investigations.

She could very well have just solved Mitch's case in the thirty seconds it had taken her to walk down the B&B's steps and the additional sixty seconds to reach this storefront. The odds were so blindingly absurd that she had to smile to herself.

"Calvin Arlos," he said with his own smile, holding out his

hand in greeting. Allie recognized his name. The report *had* mentioned that he'd owned the town's only hardware store, but he was awfully spry for recovering from having a recent heart attack. "It's nice to meet you, Ms. Delaney."

Calvin's name had been amongst the long list of suspects she'd been given. She'd learned early on in her career not to discount anyone who remained questionable, but he certainly wasn't high up on her list of possible perpetrators. She was quickly changing her opinion of him though, given that the hardware store owner was aware of details he shouldn't have normally had access to.

"How do you know who I am, if you don't mind me asking?"

Allie had reserved the last room at the B&B, and only then by sheer chance. She'd been given three nights only. Apparently, a reporter who was covering the Blyth Lake Serial Killer case was returning at that time to do a follow-up piece.

She could see why this investigation had all but taken over every regional newspaper, as well as topping out below the fold via a few nationally syndicated crime and investigation columns.

This town was picturesque with bygone oddities that were somehow still endearing.

Hadn't Mitch mentioned over the phone that at one time the only exciting thing to happen around here was when some eccentric man claimed to be abducted by aliens? It was unfortunate what had occurred since, but this case would have been yesterday's news in the papers had these murders taken place in a major city.

"Oh, everyone knows you're arriving today."

Calvin leaned down and adjusted a rather large pumpkin so that it was positioned to the right of the cornstalk. Allie almost stopped him. Should he be doing this type of physical labor given his state of health? Her gut reaction was that this man wouldn't have appreciated her pointing out his weaknesses.

"Oh, really?"

"You called Florence about a room at the inn, who in turn told Molly when you were arriving. Molly's a waitress at the diner, and I've already had my breakfast this morning. Besides, the reporters staying at the inn don't carry firearms. At least, not in holsters concealed underneath their jackets. Don't worry. It's not that noticeable. Most FBI types carry Sigs, right?"

Allie was quite proud of herself that she'd followed Calvin's logic to identify her in a long line of strangers who were probably milling about town waiting for the story to break. So much for the advantage of remaining anonymous and just an old friend of the family.

Mitch had also seen fit to give her names of shop owners and those residents who'd had any contact with the victims on a daily basis. Florence ran the day-to-day operations at the inn, and Molly was a waitress at Annie's Diner who had come into contact with practically every victim from Blyth Lake over the last two decades.

The fact that Calvin had noticed Allie's firearm wasn't unusual, though the earth-tone plaid blazer she'd chosen to wear was buttoned. Her jeans and knee-high boots topped off the perfect autumn outfit.

Allie had purposefully avoided the typical appearance of an agent in the field. She'd wanted to blend in and appear as if she were on vacation. It was quite chilly this morning, and she'd packed accordingly.

"Not a lot gets past you, does it, Mr. Arlos?" Allie gave him the compliment, all the while wondering what she was missing in this scenario. Mitch was one of the most intelligent men she had the pleasure of knowing, and she didn't doubt for a second that he would utilize the citizens in this investigation to further the development of reliable leads. So why was it taking him so long to solve this case? It should have been open and shut long ago, especially given that most of these serial killers wanted to be caught sooner or later. Recognition for one's hard work was hard to come by, and this sadistic individual had it in spades. Maybe he wasn't ready to give it up quite yet. "Oh, by the way…your cornstalk and pumpkin decorations look fantastic."

"You aren't going to ask me any questions?" Calvin inquired with a bit of confusion, reaching around in his back pocket to pull out a handkerchief to wipe his neck. He then used the white fabric to dry his hands as he studied her carefully, as if he were waiting for the other shoe to drop. "You know, about the murders up at the lake? About the people who have lived here all their lives?"

Allie could see why Mitch had been frustrated with the lock-step way Special Agent Jay Thorne had handled the investigation. He was like a bulldog putting checkmarks into little boxes to determine what came next, and no one could tell him any differently. It wasn't that the man wasn't good at his job. Quite the opposite, actually. He was very systematic and relentless in his pursuit of the truth. He closed cases quickly, moving on to the next one as if there was a prize for most cases solved in a year. Unfortunately, no one could claim he was a people person.

"I'm just in town to visit an old friend, Mr. Arlos. You all seem to be working under some false assumptions. I'm not normally a field agent, nor am I on assignment here." Allie motioned to his Halloween display to draw his attention away from the topic of conversation. She wanted these townsfolk to be comfortable around her and not believe she was analyzing every word that came out of their mouths. "I'll stop by tomorrow afternoon, though. Save me a piece of candy."

Allie might be a city girl through and through, but she was damned good at her job.

"I like you, young lady," Calvin boasted, waving a hand in the air as he turned to enter his shop. "Have a good day, and make sure you say hi to Mitch for me."

Allie continued to slowly walk down Main Street, in no rush to get to the diner. She'd told Calvin the truth in that she wasn't here on business. She was here for a friend to bounce ideas off of and talk about possibilities. She'd come to repay a personal favor. That didn't mean she couldn't enjoy this so-called time off while she was here in Small Town, USA.

When was the last time she'd taken a vacation?

Honestly, she couldn't remember when.

In fact, she'd had to look up her vacation balance before submitting her request a couple of weeks ago, because it was a required entry on the form. She'd had no idea all the days she'd accumulated over the years.

Granted, a tropical breeze with an umbrella drink in her hand might have been more relaxing than fifty or sixty-degree weather in southeastern Ohio, but she *was* paying an old debt.

Someone waved from inside the bakery, and Allie almost made a pit stop. She made a mental note to pick up a jelly donut before she left town. They were a weakness of hers, wherever she went. Seattle held claim to the trophy so far, but she was always looking for another competitor. One of the prerequisites was that the donuts had to be freshly baked or they didn't even get a shot at the crown.

She continued to take in the beautiful storefronts and all their spooky Halloween decorations, wondering if this antediluvian town was like this all year-round. The lampposts were out of the nineteen fifties, and the hand-painted windows were downright charming. The shop owners must get quite the turnout of trick or treaters with the way some of these shops adorned their display windows with seasonal decorations.

A quick glance down some of the side streets where the neighborhoods were located told the same story—this was the old-fashioned small town that everyone dreamt of raising a family in while owning a house with a white picket fence.

There was only one problem.

Allie stopped in her tracks, carefully looking around for her favorite coffee hotspot. She literally did a three-hundred-and-sixty-degree turn. She was going to join Calvin on the list of cardiac arrest patients, because there was no Starbucks anywhere to be found. For that matter, there was no large department stores, no name brand stores, and once again…no Starbucks.

How did these people survive and who would supply her IV of espresso every morning?

"You must be the sheriff's friend. I'm Deputy Byron Warner. It's nice to meet you, ma'am."

Wow. She'd been called a lot of names in her profession, but ma'am wasn't high up in the batting order.

"It's nice to meet you, as well," Allie greeted, returning the man's handshake. Deputy Warner was in uniform and holding a folder in his left hand. "I'm Alison Delaney."

She wasn't going to use her title when she shouldn't even be here in any capacity. Mitch had told her that he'd taken care of Special Agent Thorne for the time being, and she trusted her friend to do just what he promised.

This was her vacation, even if it was three years overdue.

Her thoughts kept returning to her previous discovery. How she was going to survive two weeks without her twice daily trip to Starbucks? These locals did know what an espresso was, right?

Seriously, one outlet couldn't be that far away.

Could it?

"It seems as if everyone knows who I am," Allie pointed out with a light laugh, although she was a bit uncomfortable with that knowledge. However, it did help her modify the profile she'd created on the unsub. "I was just about to walk over to the diner for some breakfast and an *espresso*. Mitch and I are meeting up at zero eight hundred."

If she hinted enough at her vital need this morning, maybe the deputy would finally give her the answer she craved.

"You're previous military?"

It appeared Calvin wasn't the only one who paid attention to things. Deputy Warner had caught on to her use of military time, something that she'd never given up. Even the FBI used twenty-four hour references in casework.

"Former military, yes," Allie answered, not comfortable with sharing anything more than that. With that said, she didn't want to appear rude. "Would you like to join us?"

"I wish I could," Byron said with an infectious grin. He had a good downhome charm to him that was hard to ignore. "I'm about to serve some search warrants up at the lake to some homeowners in regard to their boats."

"Let me guess," Allie said, sparing a glance at the police station where Agent Thorne no doubt had set up a temporary workspace for his team. She'd been in numerous investigations just like this one, though normally in a larger suburb or city. "Special Agent Thorne decided that the warrants would be better delivered by the local constabulary."

Well, look at that. It appeared that Jay Thorne *was* adapting to the town's inner workings. Would wonders never cease? Hell, maybe Mitch was having a positive effect on the agent.

Her criticism of Jay Thorne was unfair. He was a damn good agent, even though his style of investigation was completely opposite of hers. It's one of the reasons they didn't work together, though various others occurred to her in the moment.

"I won't keep you, then." Allie nodded toward Deputy Warner before realizing that he'd fallen into step with her. Had he recognized her from across the street and literally walked over to introduce himself? She had to remind herself that she wasn't in the city anymore. And she wasn't going to wait until she was old and grey to get the answer she so desperately needed. "Hey, how close is the nearest Starbucks?"

"Twenty-two miles to the east, but it's about a thirty-five-minute drive," Deputy Warner replied without hesitation. It appeared he got asked that question quite a lot. No doubt by the reporters who were used to amenities this place couldn't offer while pursuing a deadline. "We have our own café a block down that serves a mean hot chocolate with whipped cream, not to mention the best java this side of the Ohio."

Allie didn't have a thing against hot chocolate, but it wasn't espresso. Neither was coffee, really. Back in the day, a black cup of coffee would have sufficed. Now? There was nothing better than a venti caramel macchiato, triple shot, extra whip to make the busy days more bearable. She'd grown accustomed to getting what she wanted.

"You have a good day, ma'am."

Oh, this ma'am thing was going to get old real quick…especially without her fix.

Since when had she gone to a ma'am instead of a miss?

Allie paused outside the diner, taking a second to look at her reflection in the glass window. Sure enough, there were a few crow's feet around her eyes that proved Deputy Warner's point regarding the use of ma'am.

Honestly, it shouldn't matter that her eyes were still slightly bloodshot from lack of sleep. She also shouldn't care that she hadn't had time to get fresh highlights in her hair before flying out of D.C., but that didn't stop her from manipulating a thick lock that fell from the clip so that it framed her face just so— all's fair in love and war, etc., etc.

It had been over a year since she'd last seen Mitch Kendall, and she wasn't sure that was quite long enough to get him out of her system. The last time they'd met up in D.C. had ended up with both of them in the rack, both of them quickly coming to the realization that they were better off as friends then casual lovers.

It had nothing to do with the physical connection.

Truthfully, she'd never been with anyone better. It came down to neither one of them being built for commitment, and forcing themselves into that mold wouldn't have helped the situation.

Besides, it wasn't like he was even her type.

She completely blamed the tequila, considering she usually tended more toward the decidedly worthless and devilishly cute type.

She hadn't had a shot of the stuff since.

"Ma'am?" A gentleman with thinning brown hair was holding the door open for her, his smile not quite meeting his dark eyes. There was a sadness about him that had nothing to do with his obvious ailing health. "Were you going inside?"

"Yes," Allie said, returning his smile with one of her own. "Thank you."

The delicious smell of bacon immediately overwhelmed her senses, overcoming the underlying scent of grease that hung in the air. Honestly, the delectable fragrance had her stomach rumbling the moment she stepped foot across the threshold.

Allie didn't have to look to her left to know that Mitch Kendall stood there waiting for her. He'd always had a strong presence, and that was likely never to fade given the type of man he was right down to his core.

She had to remind herself that she was here as a friend, and not something more.

"No Starbucks?" Allie spoke before her gaze met Mitch's blue eyes that sparkled at her inquiry. He was just as handsome as she remembered, with his black hair cut short in that sexy military style. He'd definitely kept himself in shape, which didn't help her resolve to get in and out of this town as quickly as possible. She'd taken two weeks' vacation, but the B&B only had three days. She'd like to stick to that schedule, if possible. "You know better than to haul my ass to a place beyond civilization that doesn't cater to my caffeine addiction, Ken."

She'd purposefully used the nickname she'd come up for him back when they'd both been in the service. He was the spitting image of the original Ken doll, with the exception of the jet-black hair and a hell of a lot more muscle.

The tag had stuck, though.

Her nickname for him had made the rounds, and the entire unit had been calling him by that name by the time they were done with that deployment. The only difference was that most of them had used it in reference to his last name, while it had a completely different meaning between them.

"Allie." Mitch patiently waited for her at the booth he'd confiscated in the back, his confidence practically emanating from every contour of his body. The minute she stepped into range, he gently pulled her into his embrace for a heartwarming hug. Damn, if his familiar touch didn't bring back a few uncomfortable memories. "It's good to see you."

"You, too," Allie whispered honestly, thinking back to better times. She gradually pulled away without looking at him to regain her professional composure. She took the seat with her back facing the door, much to her chagrin. No one in law enforcement ever put their back toward the entrance of a room, but Mitch had already commandeered the other side of the booth with his jacket and a sage green Stetson Gallatin. And just like that, she also recalled those annoying little habits that had caused them to be better friends than lovers. "I'm sorry it has to be under such unpleasant circumstances, though."

"Are you one of those frou-frou coffee drinkers that survive on sugar?" The question came out of nowhere from a waitress, and one who could only be Molly. Allie's guess had nothing to do with Calvin's mention of the woman and everything to do with the nametag pinned to her uniform. "Mitch's sister has one of those cappuccino machines over at her new office one block down, if you want something fancier. All we got here is black coffee from grounds."

"Any coffee will do at this point," Allie replied, just wanting the caffeine. "Thank you."

"She'll have what I'm having," Mitch said to the waitress, already lifting his cup to his lips. His blue gaze met hers right before he revealed something personal to a complete stranger. He'd also slid right into that zone that they'd both agreed never to return again. "Allie likes her eggs scrambled, though."

"I see you haven't changed, Ken." Allie unbuttoned her beige plaid blazer, which happened to be one of her favorites. After leaving the Marines so many years ago, she'd had to change her battle dress uniform. Today, she was on vacation. And besides, if she was going to eat a big breakfast, she'd better make room for it. She completely ignored the zing of pleasure that shot through her at the fact that he remembered how she liked her eggs. "You didn't tell me that I was going to be taken back to the 1700s. Are there any scheduled witch trials coming up?"

"More like 1950s, but trust me…it grows on you," Mitch said with a fond smile, telling her everything she needed to know. He loved this town and everything it stood for—apple pies, Farmall tractors, and trustworthy city elders. He raised his lashes so that he was staring directly at her, allowing her to witness his frustration before he set his mug on the table. "Allie, these folks are scared. I'm at a loss here, because every lead we get turns into dust in the light of day. My family is getting drug deeper and deeper into this mess, and I can't seem to do a damned thing about fixing it. The feds aren't having much luck figuring this case out, either."

"I'm just another one of those feds," Allie gently reminded him, wishing she had better news to share that could end this investigation in a matter of minutes. Unfortunately, they were dealing with an unsub who had over ten years to perfect his craft. There *was* a silver lining, but she wasn't sure Mitch was ready to hear it. "I don't have a magic wand that I can twirl in my hand and make an arrest, Ken."

"No, but having you here in the bullpen can allow the profile to be modified instantly. You'll be able to notice when vital elements stick out. You can be the key that will unlock this entire investigation. You said yourself that you work better inside the killer's own safety net. Thorne's profiler back at Quantico still hasn't restructured his summary based on the personal letters this psychotic nut is sending to one of the reporters, let alone taken into account the attack he made on my sister this past weekend."

Mitch kept his voice low as he continued to vent his frustration, most likely because he didn't want the patrons of the diner to overhear their conversation. Allie didn't doubt that he was aware these residents were an asset, but he couldn't ignore the truth—someone amongst these good people was a sadistic serial killer waiting to make his move and capitalize on their mistakes.

Allie had known the moment she'd amended the unsub's profile what could draw him out from hiding in the darkness, but that meant staying longer than she'd intended. She'd hold the ace close to her chest and hope that something else came to her in the next thirty-six hours.

Honestly, she was surprised that Mitch hadn't seen the tarot card set before him.

Allie was the unsub's ideal victim.

She was the Empress.

CHAPTER FOUR

"**R**EADY TO SEE my hometown of Blyth Lake?" Mitch asked as he held open the door to the diner so that Allie could step outside. "It's beautiful this time of year. Our fall colors are in their full glory right now."

Truthfully, Mitch didn't want to take the time to show Allie his hometown. He had numerous questions regarding the revised profile she'd modified from the original one they'd developed on the serial killer. The unsub seemed to have made it his personal mission to target the Kendalls.

Mitch wanted answers.

He needed to understand why, and his patience had worn thin from the day he'd arrived back in town.

Unfortunately, it had been close to a year since he'd last seen Allie in person. She was still as naturally beautiful as the day he'd met her sixteen years ago. She wore less makeup than any other female he knew. Yes, they'd fallen into bed one weekend after having too many drinks, but they'd both quickly realized that was a surefire way to ruin a lasting friendship.

It was hard to believe that he'd known her for so long.

Allie had been part of the roster of Marines on his first deployment on a Marine Expeditionary Unit (MEU), though she'd worked intelligence for S-3 operations. Her dedication and commitment to serving her country as a Marine had earned his undying respect, but it was her intellectual capacity and compassion for those they served with that had netted his loyalty beyond their time in the service together.

"Don't give me that horseshit." Allie squinted at the bright rays of the morning sun as they stepped outside from the diner. She didn't bother to walk in either direction as she called him out on his insincere offer to show her around town. "You want to know if my profile on your unsub has significantly changed."

Mitch didn't hesitate to hand over his aviator sunglasses he'd hung from the neck of his buttoned-down shirt. The traditional October chill seeped down to the bone this morning, and he was glad that he'd grabbed his brown leather bomber jacket from the house as he left for the station this morning. Allie was smart enough to have worn a dark turtleneck underneath her blazer.

"You already have the case files, Allie." Mitch was grateful that Allie hadn't let him get away with too much small talk. "Did anything alter your view after the events of this past weekend? This son of a bitch had the balls to attack my sister. Gwen doesn't even have a thread of hair in common with the other victims, so why risk trying to abduct her from her own home?"

"I believe I have a few answers for you, but I'd like to hear every detail from the beginning…possibly walk the ground." Allie held up her hand when Mitch would have protested. Couldn't she see that this was a waste of time? "I want to hear the facts from you directly, not from some politically biased reports that were written up to cover someone's ass. Or worse yet, from some inexperienced newbie and his retired on active duty supervisor who would rather put his feet up at the station. And when I say the beginning, I mean from before you ever arrived into town to take over as sheriff. I want to know everything about this unsub from the first incident here in his hometown to the latest attack on your sister."

Mitch bit back the objection that wanted to erupt from his

chest. Allie didn't know it, but she represented his last best hope. His family had won a few battles recently, but in truth…it felt as if they were losing the war in the face of this fiend and his latest bold attack.

Allie was a refreshing breath of crisp country air, and he needed to inhale deeper and longer than he'd thought possible. She was an old friend who he'd basically blackmailed to help him with this case, but she was also a reminder of the past that he didn't want to lose.

They'd tried their hand ever so briefly at something more, with both of them quickly realizing what a mistake that would be given the circumstances at the time.

They were too different back then, both of them heading in opposite directions.

She was a dyed in the wool city girl through and through.

He was as pure country as a blue tick coonhound, and he belonged right here in Blyth Lake.

Mitch had told everyone that the sheriff's assignment that he received upon his homecoming was temporary, because he'd thought his retirement would contain something completely different from his past.

He'd been dead wrong, and his previous assumptions had been untrue.

His parents had both been born here in Blyth Lake, and his mother had died lying in her own bed in the home she'd created with his father. They'd both loved everything about this town, and it was now Mitch's duty to see to it that their hometown was looked after.

He took his responsibilities as its protector very seriously.

"Allie, this is a complete waste of time." Mitch didn't want to rehash something he'd gone over a thousand times already. Even the smallest detail had been catalogued into those reports.

He'd made sure of it by including addendums and updating an extensive photographic catalogue of every aspect of the crime scenes, including the underwater coverage of the killing ground at the bottom of the lake. Nothing he said would change or alter the facts of this case. "I even emailed you yesterday my sister's account of what transpired Sunday night after she got home from our family dinner. This monster orchestrated it so that he could get her alone at the house. It took planning, cunningness, and downright manipulation of many people to reach her without any witnesses."

It was clear that Allie wasn't going to debate with him. She'd made up her mind to hear him repeat the case history in person. Nothing he said or did would get him access to her profile until he began talking about the most important case he'd ever worked.

She'd settled the aviator sunglasses on the bridge of her nose, not caring that they were a little too big for her features. Her chestnut colored hair had been pulled back into a bun of some sort, yet the style came off as casual. After all, she was on vacation. She could have been a local given a few more days to blend in, yet the way she carried herself gave off a city vibe.

He'd missed her.

The thought came out of nowhere, and she'd caught him staring at her.

"Ken?"

Allie lowered the sunglasses to see if he was paying attention, peering up at him with brown eyes that had the most unusual green flecks he'd ever seen. He really needed to get his head on straight, or he'd screw this up, too.

"I want to hear from you everything that took place in this town *before* I give you the updated profile I amended on the plane last night." Allie gave a light shrug when she pushed the glasses back up the bridge of her nose. "There's something I want to check first, and I'm not comfortable giving you the file without confirming it myself. Technically, it shouldn't even exist. I could lose my job over meddling in this, Ken."

"I'd never let that happen, Allie." Mitch hadn't spent the last sixteen years in the Corps without making quite a few connections with people still in a position of power. Allie had only served five years in the intelligence field in the Corps before heading off for college and joining the FBI. They'd stayed in touch through it all—emails, texts, and phone calls. A lot had changed in the Marines since she'd gotten out, and he'd worked his way up to Gunnery Sergeant before being forced out due to medical reasons. He knew people who knew the right people. That's all that mattered in this situation. "Just tell me what it is you need to know. I'll confirm or deny it right now."

"You've always been impatient, haven't you?"

Mitch rubbed his mouth with his hand to prevent himself from denying her claim. There was one area where he had the patience of a saint, and she was well aware of that fact. It was best not to bring up their intimate past, so he let her comment slide.

Allie was here strictly because he'd asked her…and for the right kind of business purposes only. Besides, they were a hell of a lot better off as friends.

"You hated calling in that chip, didn't you?" Allie asked softly, buttoning her jacket as if she only now realized that her firearm was showing. Another strand of hair had come out of the bun at the base of her neck and formed a curl next to her cheek as she peered down at the button. It was as if she couldn't look at him while he answered. The thing of it was, he didn't want to reply to her question. "Ken, you saved my life back then. There's no question that I owe you everything, but I'm not here because of that. I'm here because that's what friends do for one another. So, keep that favor you'll need tucked away in your back pocket and know that you can still use it sometime in the future."

Mitch was prevented from responding to her tempting offer when Tobias Essinger turned the corner of Third Street. He was carrying one of the western books he loved so much in his right hand, clearly not expecting someone to be right around the corner.

"Sheriff, I'm so sorry. I wasn't watching where I was going." Tobias looked over his shoulder, as if someone was following him. "Maybe it's a good thing I bumped into you. You should know that I think I saw someone skulking around Chad Schaeffer's house, but I know he's not home. Maybe it's his father?"

Mitch had seen Miles Schaeffer sitting at the counter with Harlan Whitmore and Chester Mayer. No, Chad's father wasn't over at his son's house.

"It's good to have neighbors like you, Tobias," Mitch responded, purposefully remaining relaxed as the conversation progressed. He wasn't about to have the older gentleman believe that someone was actually breaking in to Chad's place. The entire community would be up in arms, and he wasn't going to allow that to happen unless there was some truth behind Tobias' claims. "Maybe Chad has someone checking on his house while he stays with Gwen. I'll tell you what. I'll give Chad a call while Allie and I head that way. We'll make sure the coast is clear."

"It's nice to meet you, young lady. I hope you can help catch this son of a bitch who's all but turned our town into a headline for the nightly news," Tobias grumbled, his grip tightening on his hardback western book. "Did you see that reporter on television last night? She all but suggested that your sister wasn't happy here in Blyth Lake. Why, that piece of—"

"I did catch Charlene Winston's clip," Mitch advised Tobias, wanting to wrap this up quickly so that he and Allie could check out Chad's property. "We can't control the media, so it's best to ignore the reports. You go on and enjoy your breakfast, Tobias. Try not to dwell on the newscast. All that accomplishes is putting us all in bad moods."

Allie stepped to the side with a warm smile, nodding at Tobias as he walked past them. She waited until he was out of earshot to speak her mind.

"What do we have here, Ken? Don't you have one of those radios these small towns use to communicate with your deputies?" Allie peered down Third Street, but she waited for him to decide. She must really be lacking in the caffeine department, because this wasn't her normal disposition. "And isn't Chad Schaeffer the man involved with your sister?"

"Yes, which is why I'm well aware that he isn't home at the moment."

"And Miles Schaeffer was at the counter of Annie's Diner enjoying what appeared to be biscuits and gravy with a side of bacon," Allie tacked on, tilting her head to the side while she waited for his decision. He regretted handing over his sunglasses, because all he was doing was staring back at his own reflection. "So, what's it going to be, Ken? Do we go in with guns blazing?"

"Funny. By the way, do I want to know how you identified Miles Schaeffer as one of the men at the counter?" Mitch didn't want to waste any time, so he began to walk briskly down Third Street. He scanned the various properties they passed once they got deeper into the residential neighborhood. Each house was decorated with pumpkins, makeshift graveyards, and an occasional haunted yard for those folks who went out of their way for the trick or treaters to enjoy the holiday. "I don't recall sending you pictures along with those names."

"If I told you all my secrets, then you'd be an agent and wouldn't even need my help." Allie wiggled her eyebrows behind his sunglasses, keeping up with each long stride he took. "Which house is Schaeffer's? More importantly, why aren't you going to radio this in?"

Mitch didn't want to admit that he *did* have one of those small radios, but he'd left it at the station. She'd make some quip about him being the local Barney Fife, and he wasn't in the mood for that type of banter right now.

Besides, Patty had his cell phone number.

Should anything of relevance occur, she and the other deputies knew how to reach him and vice versa. He wouldn't be calling anything in until he knew for certain a crime had been committed.

"Hey," Allie said softly after she'd removed his sunglasses and causally rested a hand on his arm. Her gesture brought him to a halt in the middle of the sidewalk. "I didn't mean to make fun of your team. Listen, Tobias is one of those neighbors who keeps an eye on things, and he believes he saw someone out of place. You gave me his information in one of the files. From what I remember, there isn't a resident in this town that he doesn't know. That means either he witnessed an individual he's not familiar with breaking into Chad Schaeffer's residence or Tobias' imagination is working overtime for…"

Mitch realized that he'd gotten so caught up in the residents as if they were his own family that he wasn't succeeding at compartmentalizing the information Tobias had shared with them. It didn't help that his baby sister had been attacked in her own home recently.

"Because he ruminated over Charlene Winston's clip last night on the eleven o'clock news." Mitch hated being made a fool of, and he'd succeeded in doing just that. This case was personal, and he was now becoming a Tobias Essinger. "We should still check it out."

"We should. One can never be too careful," Allie readily agreed, handing over his sunglasses with a smile. She no longer needed them since the sun wasn't directly in their eyes. "It's rare I get to go into the field, Ken. A little excitement isn't such a bad thing."

Mitch shook his head at her ability to cover up his overreaction, but he still wouldn't be satisfied until he was one hundred percent certain that someone hadn't broken into Schaeffer's residence.

It didn't take them long to reach Chad's home.

Sure enough, there wasn't any sign of a break-in.

Had Tobias' mind been playing tricks on him?

Allie was the profiler. She'd hit the nail on the head, but again…he needed concrete proof that nothing was disturbed either outside or inside Schaeffer's house.

Allie had gone around the back of the property, while Mitch located the spare key underneath one of the rocks near the front step of the porch. He'd have to speak with Chad about the lack of safety in such an obvious hiding spot, but it was the way things had been done in Blyth Lake for years.

Unfortunately, times had changed.

A quick search of the house revealed that nothing was out of place.

It was a relief to step out onto the small porch and see one of the younger teens running through the yard, probably coming back from one of his friend's house. The local school was on fall break, meaning no classes yesterday, today, or tomorrow. Thursday would resume as normal, but the teen's route of travel between houses was most likely what Tobias had noticed as being unusual.

"It's good to know your skills are as sharp as ever," Mitch praised once Allie came around the corner. She had a grace to her that reminded him of his mother, not that he'd ever say that aloud. Allie would definitely take his compliment the wrong way. It appeared as if he didn't have to say a thing to offend her, because her frown spoke volumes. "Allie?"

Something was wrong.

"No," Allie said, abruptly holding up her hand to stop him from walking past her. "Don't. Everything's fine."

"No, everything isn't fine." Mitch closed the distance between them, looking over her shoulder toward the back of the property to see what could have warranted such a judgmental reaction. "What did you find back there?"

"Mitch, this town…" Allie looked up and down the neighborhood street in what seemed to be disbelief. It was then he noticed that she wasn't upset so much as taken aback. "Look around you. People have their garage doors open. Flimsy screens are in the windows. Nothing is locked. Some even have nothing but screened doors to allow the cool air into their homes, without any thought that someone could walk inside without the slightest hesitation."

Mitch relaxed somewhat. He'd said it before, but she was city all the way clear to her obsession with having a coffee place on every corner. She wasn't used to country folks who trusted in their neighbors to do the right thing, which included making their own coffee.

"Allie, these people grew up in a time when locking doors wasn't something you needed to do unless you were leaving the house to go on vacation. Trust me when I say that they *have* started to take more precautions, but they aren't going to change their perception of their neighbors overnight."

"Well, you better hold some type of town meeting soon," Allie suggested seriously, her brows practically touching as she did one more scan of the neighborhood. "A town like Blyth Lake is a serial killer's dream, and he's not going to give it up without a fight."

CHAPTER FIVE

A LLIE WALKED ALONG the perimeter of the fence as the cool breeze brushed past her face, wicking away her body heat. She could hear the rustle of the golden leaves in the trees above moving against one another as the gentle wind came through the meadow to her right. Every now and then she'd hear beautiful songs of various birds as they readied themselves for the approaching winter and their migration south.

It was hard to believe that such a peaceful plot of land existed while a serial killer stalked his prey less than a few miles away.

"You're a very lucky man, Ken."

"You don't have to tell me that," Mitch replied, falling into step beside her after he'd disconnected a call with Deputy Warner. The warrants his office had executed to search the various boats docked on personal property at the behest of the FBI hadn't gone over as well as Agent Thorne had expected, even though they'd been conducted by a local. That wasn't much of a surprise to anyone involved. "I've been fortunate to have my family, and even more so to have been blessed with two loving parents."

Allie ignored the sharp pierce of envy she always experienced whenever anyone mentioned family. She hadn't been so lucky in that department, but she was never one to dwell on the past. She steeled herself with an eye toward the future.

Allie continued to walk along the aging barbed wire fence

line, breathing in the fresh autumn air. There was an intoxicating scent that couldn't be found in D.C. Autumn was definitely in the air. Mitch had decided that a walk through his small town was no longer needed, so he'd all but escorted her to the sheriff's car.

She kept to herself that maybe an upgrade in vehicles was due, considering the buttons and switches on the dashboard could have been from the 1950s he'd spoken of earlier. He'd witnessed her disbelief before giving her a brief explanation that Deputy Warner was currently driving the SUV the town had authorized for the sheriff's department.

That one thoughtful act told Allie how much Mitch cared for his deputies.

"Could you please do me a favor and finally start from the beginning?" Allie asked, not needing to turn her head to see the frown she knew would be on his face.

Mitch didn't want to waste any more time.

She understood his impatience, but she wasn't like some of the other profilers employed by the FBI. Her colleagues could look at a case file and whip something out for the lead agent in a matter of a couple days. She'd done it herself more times than she could count, but she personally liked to get an up close and personal read of the investigation.

"We were interrupted before, but I wouldn't be asking you if I didn't feel it was important," Allie pressed once more. "We need a fresh perspective."

Mitch had driven her out to his new place, which she had to admit was absolutely stunning. The land was positioned right at the entrance of town, giving any passerby a view of vast acres of rolling pastures, a barn that must have been a staple of the property since the early part of the century, and a beautiful farmhouse that was meant for a larger family.

She'd never pictured Mitch as a family man, because the individual standing before her didn't like to commit to anything other than having his team's backs, or six as they called it in the service. Yes, he took his duties of protecting this town just as seriously as he had when securing the freedom of this country in distant lands…but there was something different about him now that she couldn't pinpoint.

"We're only wasting time," Mitch argued, bringing her attention back around to the conversation at hand. He leaned down to grab a stick that had been directly in his path, telling her that some of the attributes in his fierce demeanor still existed. "Agent Thorne is probably up at the lake right now, scouring through my neighbors' boats moored to private docks. Byron is up there to make sure the residents are placated, but it's not going to be enough. We're all missing something that's key to bringing this son of a bitch down."

"Jay got the warrant, and he had probable cause to do so or he wouldn't have been able to get the judge to sign it," Allie said in defense of an agent that she didn't particularly like. No one could argue the man's closing rate on these types of investigations. It was rather impressive. "The individual you're looking for is right here amongst the residents—someone you've seen most of your life and thought you knew. The unsub is male, most likely in his early to late thirties, experienced a loss of a parent early on in his life, and truly believes he's doing something right by his victims in killing these young girls. He's grouping them together, providing them a makeshift family plot with that gravesite you discovered in the lake."

"You're not telling me anything Thorne's profiler hasn't already written down in some case file somewhere, but I've also witnessed you in the field. When we were looking for that sniper in that village in Iraq—the shooter who was taking our guys out one by one. You were able to identify him within three days of us arriving at that village."

"I'm not a miracle worker, Ken. And I wasn't even a profiler back then. I was an analyst. It was just common sense. A process of elimination that I used to weed out the possibilities in order to identity of the sniper."

Allie had known early on what she'd wanted to do with her life, and she'd entered the military with a clear goal in mind. The FBI favored those applicants with military backgrounds, especially those with defined close-in-weapons skills and field experience so that they could hit the ground running. It also hadn't hurt that the military had taken her away from a not-so-good home domestic situation.

"We're dealing with a serial killer who has his own personal hunting ground here in the surrounding counties. To pick up anything different than the profiler Jay has been relying on will require me to see or hear something that's not in the reports. Some hint of a clue that everyone else had dismissed as meaningless."

"Every damn detail is in those damn reports," Mitch muttered, his frustration shining through as bright as the sun overhead.

"Not everything." Allie couldn't help but lean down and pick up the most beautiful, perfect fall leaf she'd ever seen. It was fire-red with streaks of gold through the center. She twirled it by the stem to show Mitch that she wasn't in the same hurry he was. He'd been through a lot since returning home and it showed. It would do him good to slow down and process everything that had taken place in such a short amount of time. "Nowhere in those reports did it say that the majority of the town's inhabitants leave their garage doors open in the middle of the day or the fact that they don't bother to secure their front doors, leaving them unlocked for anyone to stroll right on in to get a look into their private lives."

"And that makes a difference how? These people all know virtually every detail about every soul in this town. Nothing is sacred."

"And that's where you're wrong. Mitch, I'll answer your question if you walk me through the entire case," Allie responded, having more confidence that she'd get what she needed from this conversation by the time Mitch needed to return to the station. "You have my word."

"Fine." Mitch tossed the branch into the air, letting it sail into the wind far away from the fence. He didn't miss a beat. "Noah was the first to return to town. My brother was taking out a wall in his new house to redecorate when it was discovered that a body had been enclosed in the drywall. The victim was Sophia Morton, a young girl who'd once attended a summer camp here twelve years ago and developed some friendships here locally."

"Noah and the rest of the town firmly believed the body belonged to Emma Irwin, though," Allie pointed out as she stepped over a divot in the freshly cut grass. They were getting pretty far from the house, but it was better to keep walking while they talked. Mitch was bound to reveal more details that would help her adjust the profile needed to catch the individual who'd been terrorizing this town for over a decade. "Emma had gone missing from a bonfire...around this same time of year, I believe."

"Yes. And we found Emma's remains with the rest of the young women who have gone missing over the years. So why seal up Sophia's body?"

Allie debated giving Mitch her theories now, and she decided that it would keep this conversation rolling in the right direction if she didn't interrupt. Besides, it would give her a little more time to enjoy this beautiful weather. It was doubtful she'd have time to experience anything like this after returning to work in a couple of weeks.

"I believe the unsub was interrupted or feared discovery. We'll probably never know if Emma or Sophia was the first victim unless we capture the unsub. The underlying connection is that all of the young girls had publicly expressed being unhappy at home at one point or another. Even the simplest of complaints could have led this unsub into believing they were miserable in their current domestic situation. He feels he's helping them reconnect with another soul."

"By killing them?"

"By taking away the pain of their difficult lives and giving them a family of their own...by him making them immortal together as a group."

"Then how do you explain the death of Deputy Wallace?"

"This unsub has never had to deal with uncertainty. He's at home here in Blyth Lake. This is where he feels secure." Allie turned so that she was walking backward and able to study Mitch's expressions, needing him to understand why the killer was the way he was. "Noah discovering Sophia's body was the first time the unsub encountered uncertainty. He most likely put Sophia out of his mind and made himself forget that he'd abandoned her there in that wall."

"Noah made him rash and angry," Mitch surmised, rubbing his jaw as he considered her version of what could have taken place the night Deputy Wallace had been killed next to his patrol vehicle. "I can see that. And we've kept him running from that point on, reacting to our probes into his world."

"I believe the unsub returned to the old Yoder farm the night Deputy Wallace was killed. He was there to right a wrong."

Allie could see that Mitch was no longer impatient to get back into town. That was a good sign. She needed his disposition to be open, to be receptive to where she was going with this conversation. "The unsub's goal was to take Sophia to the lake and have her join her sisters. Deputy Wallace had been asked to patrol the property, but the unsub must have gotten complacent and didn't expect anyone to be lurking about. I believe he was there to take care of his so-called family member who he'd abandoned."

"I guess that rules out…" Mitch finally caught on. He slid his large hand around to the back of his neck. No doubt, he had a lot of tension built up trying to solve this case and keep the residents of this town safe. "You thought Byron Warner was the guilty party."

"No," Allie corrected him, taking a few steps before deciding she wanted to stop their walk. She leaned an elbow on the worn wooden fencepost. "I don't think in terms of individuals at this point, but I do take into consideration the characteristics of the profile. Byron is of the right age, he knows this town better than he knows the back of his hand, and the residents trust him with their secrets. Do I believe it's Byron Warner? No, I don't. He was raised by two parents who loved and supported him his entire life. That alone would scratch his name off the list. So, what happened after Deputy Wallace was murdered for being in the wrong place at the wrong time?"

"Sheriff Percy was basically forced to resign from his position, because he wasn't properly supervising his deputies. Percy didn't run a very tight ship. Due to his negligence, Wallace died all alone out there."

"And then?"

"Lance arrived back in town, discovering old Polaroid photographs of all the victims in the house my parents gave him. At least, the ones we know about thus far. That led Detective Kendrick, who was lead on the investigation until such time that the feds took over, to believe that Harlan Whitmore might be involved with the killings."

Allie recalled reading Harlan's interview, but she didn't believe that the older gentleman was the unsub for many different reasons.

"Lance is the youngest of your brothers?"

"Yes." Mitch took her lead and leaned against a solid post in the fence line that was sturdy compared to some of the others down this section. He crossed his arms and studied her with those sparkling blue eyes that got her every damn time. "I'm the oldest. It goes in the order of me, Gwen, Jace, Noah, and then Lance. We grew up with both parents, we all had a happy childhood, and we even came back home after we'd sowed our wild oats in the service. So, tell me why Gwen would be a target?"

"Not until we finish the rest of the timeline." Allie continued to twirl the leaf in between her fingers, ignoring the fact that frustration was once again written across his features. She liked it more when he wasn't so tense. "Harlan Whitmore might have been the realtor on all the properties involved this far into the story, but Miles Schaeffer and his sons also worked on all of those houses. At least, enough to get the homes in a livable condition. Wasn't it Clayton who attempted to burn down Lance's residence to cover up the fact that he'd been the one who rebuilt the staircase that led to the basement?"

"Yes, but Detective Kendrick ruled out Clayton as a suspect for numerous reasons."

"We're not done with the Kendalls' involvement, though. Jace then returned to town and fell in love with Shae Irwin, Emma's older sister." Allie ignored the way Mitch's features began to morph with fury, continuing with the events that occurred after the middle brother's homecoming. She wasn't accusing Jace of anything, and Mitch would soon realize that. "The unsub immediately focused on her."

"Which led the authorities to find the killer's gravesite, which brought in the feds."

"Along with you," Allie stated, now getting to the more substantial information that would eventually be the downfall of a serial killer. "The unsub then retreated back into the shadows. Everything that he's worked so hard for over the course of his life with these girls was taken from him, and there was a Kendall family member at every turn. The unsub's makeshift family had been taken away from him one by one…by *your* family."

"Fuck," Mitch muttered, looking away from her and into the distance. He was visualizing himself what the unsub must have experienced. "Every one of my siblings inadvertently had a hand in the unraveling of this case."

"Yes," Allie confirmed, taking a deep breath and giving Mitch her final conclusion. "The unsub is also grieving. He lost his family. One of the bodies you discovered in the lake was identified as Pamela Graber. When Gwen moved into Pamela's house, I believe he was using Gwen as a substitute for the sister who'd been taken away from him. It was why he spray painted the words *Welcome Home* on the side of the barn."

"So, when Gwen didn't move in right away, but instead stayed with Dad…"

"The unsub couldn't reach out to your sister, so he chose to utilize a reporter who would no doubt print whatever he wrote for her. Charlene Winston became his voice for all to hear, which then evolved into something else."

"Because he was able to tell his story," Mitch finished for her with a shake of his head. "All this time I believed he was taunting us. Is it your belief that he attacked Gwen in her home to take her up to the lake? That makes no sense, especially given that we're monitoring that area frequently."

"The unsub went to a lot of trouble to gain access to Gwen. He risked a great deal doing what he did. There could be a few reasons for that, but I won't know until he shows another card. He might have even found himself a new gravesite to gather his new victims. As I stated earlier, we're looking for a male in his early to mid-thirties whose family life consisted of one parent. He blends in easily among the residents and displays concern for those who need advice. He's probably never been married and even has trouble maintaining a serious relationship due to his obsession with the family of his own creation."

Allie spent most of her time behind a desk, combing over evidence and intelligence to form an accurate profile on individuals who ranged from terrorists to serial killers. It was rare that she was able to go into the field to see the ground involved in these stories.

"I'm here as a personal favor, which limits the capacity in which I can work." Allie didn't believe for one second that Agent Thorne had given her visit his blessing. "But I can use those confines to my benefit."

"I don't understand." It was easy to see that Mitch's thoughts were racing in several different directions at once after the information she'd just dumped on him. His first instinct was probably to get back to the station, read through the letters the unsub has been sending to Charlene Winston, and go through the personal lives of every male between the ages of thirty and forty who never been married and grew up with just one parent. "Are you thinking you'll be able to blend in while you're here, thus allowing the residents to open up to you in a way they wouldn't with Agent Thorne? That remains to be seen."

"Yes, that's exactly what I was hoping for, to be honest." Allie could have expanded on her answer, but Mitch would have immediately shut her down. Hell, he might have actually sent her packing. But he'd called in this favor, and she was here to see it through. Truthfully, concentrating on bringing a serial killer to justice was probably healthier than acting on the thoughts that had all but consumed her since she'd crossed the county line. "Should we head back into town? I'm thinking maybe a small shopping spree is in order while you go help Agent Thorne with the more troublesome search warrants."

Allie decided to keep the leaf. Maybe she'd press it in a book for a keepsake. Nature was always more beautiful in the country than the city, but maybe that was just her skewed perception of things.

She'd only taken a single step when Mitch stopped her from walking back to the house.

"Thank you for coming here, Allie." Mitch appeared as if he wanted to say more. He didn't have to tell her how important it was for him to safeguard these people he'd sworn to protect. He hadn't materially changed in all the years she'd known him, with the exception of now owning a house meant for a huge family. He gave her a small smile. "You know I'm impatient when it comes to bureaucracy and getting right down to it."

"Then you should have chosen another profession, Ken." Allie breathed a little easier when Mitch dropped his hand from her arm. A little space would go a long way in maintaining the friendship they'd built over the years. "Sheriff of your hometown? Really?"

Mitch shrugged good-naturedly as he began to walk back toward his beautiful new home. She'd never seen anything more stunning than the two-story farmhouse set just inside the town's limits. He could see who was coming and going by simply having a seat on his front porch watching life move along in this small town in middle America.

"It's what Blyth Lake needed from me, and you know I have trouble saying no."

Allie laughed and purposefully bumped her shoulder into his arm to prove her point. That's what a friend would do, right?

"You never had a problem saying no before now. Remember when Chaz wanted you to cover for him with the CO? I believe you announced at formation to the entire unit that Chaz would be out of commission for the day because he was busy shaving his balls to get rid of the crabs he'd picked up socializing with the…ladies in the ville. Though, I also believe you were a bit more eloquent than that, if I remember correctly."

"That's the price that he needed be pay for his earlier indiscretions and their consequences," Mitch said, returning Allie's laugh with one of his own. "He shirked his duties because he'd gotten lit up the night before playing in a poker game with another unit."

"Exactly," Allie pointed out, catching sight of a vehicle driving up the gravel lane. It appeared that Mitch had an unexpected visitor. "Chaz didn't have sex that night, and he didn't have a case of the crabs. You fabricated the whole story to teach him a lesson, in spite of the fact that he asked you to cover for him."

"Yeah, well, my dad wasn't the one asking for the favor at the time," Mitch said somewhat distractedly as he gazed at the approaching vehicle. He purposefully shifted his steps so that he was to the right of Allie. She didn't have to be a profiler to know he'd done so with the inherent need to protect her flank. Whoever was driving the beat-up old Chevy truck wasn't a trusted friend. "Allie, I believe that you're about to meet your first possible suspect."

CHAPTER SIX

"**J**ACK, WHAT BRINGS you out my way?"

Mitch warily regarded Jack Stewart as the man got out of his Chevy pickup truck. He was Molly's son and currently dating Beth Ann Mason. He'd grown up locally without a father for much of his childhood, had close ties to the community, and had never maintained a relationship longer than six months.

Did Jack's current relationship with Beth Ann disqualify him from the suspect pool?

"I'm heading into the city, but I thought I'd stop by and let you know that Shelby is setting up some type of antennae behind the welcome sign coming into town," Jack said, leaning against his open door. Mitch didn't miss the way Jack's gaze perused Allie, just as it was also noticeable he was using his right arm to rest against the metal ridge. The killer had been grazed with a bullet to the left arm, courtesy of Mitch's sister. "Patty wasn't picking up at the station, and your house is on my way out of town."

That was code for wanting to check out the latest visitor to grace Blyth Lake. Jack had no doubt stopped in at the diner and gotten the latest gossip about Allie Delaney and their conversation from earlier. He probably was telling the truth about heading into the city, but this brief stop would garner what information he could for the rest of the crowd still milling about town looking for an update—Billy Stanton, Julie Brigham, Beth

Ann Mason, and the list went on.

What was worrisome to Mitch was the fact that Patty hadn't picked up the telephone at the station. Jack wouldn't have lied about that, given the circumstances they all faced.

"Jack? You must be Molly's son. She spoke very highly of you this morning." Allie stepped forward and held out her right arm in greeting. She'd been holding the autumn leaf in her left hand for some time, and she didn't seem inclined to give it up anytime soon. "I'm Allie Delaney, a friend of Mitch's from our time back in the Corps."

"You were in the Marines?" Jack's astonishment was the typical reaction from a civilian upon learning that Allie was a former jarhead. It was the soft quality in her mannerisms that made even Mitch sometimes forget that she'd served by his side during a number of tours off and on for nearly five years. "I'd heard you were a fed, but a Marine? Now that's just badass."

"I'll take that as a compliment," Allie replied with a light laugh that set Mitch on edge. What the hell did she think she was doing flirting with one of the local suspects? She knew damn well from the reports he'd provided her that Jack was dating Beth Ann, but the man fit her profile in every other aspect. "The Marines gave me a sense of purpose at the young, impressionable age of eighteen. You know how it is to be raised by a single parent, right? The options are somewhat limited, to say the least."

It took a moment for Mitch to comprehend what Allie had just done and how it correlated back to their conversation not five minutes prior to Jack's arrival.

Son of a bitch.

Allie was purposefully making herself a target, filling out the victim's profile.

Well, she could take that idea and waltz her little ass right out of town. That wasn't the reason he'd called in his favor, and he sure as hell wasn't going to be the reason she became a target or lost her life after everything he'd done to make sure she had one all those years ago.

"How's Beth Ann doing, Jack?"

"Beth Ann?" Jack's gaze finally switched to Mitch, who purposefully stared him down with a warning more obvious than the bright sun shining overhead. "She's great. It's really working out for her over at your sister's place."

"That's good to know." Mitch gestured toward Jack that it was time for him to leave, and that his five minutes were up. He struggled to come up with a good reason for approaching Jack, maybe even slapping him on the left upper arm in a friendly manner to see if he winced in reaction. Would there be a wound on his upper left arm? "I appreciate the courtesy drive-by. I'll have Byron do another welfare check on Shelby, and I'll find out why Patty wasn't picking up the main line over at the station."

"Glad I could be of help," Jack said, nodding in Allie's direction before hopping back into the cab of his truck. Within seconds, he had his left elbow out the window as was his usual habit. Had there been a wince that crossed the man's features due to such a casual movement? "I'm sure I'll see the two of you at The Cavern later this week."

Mitch gave Jack a tight smile that never reached his eyes and waited for him to pull out of the drive. He was quite proud of himself for waiting until the dust cleared before turning on Allie and calling her out on the transparent plan to draw the serial killer out of hiding.

"What the hell was that horseshit all about?" Mitch all but demanded, turning to confront her.

Allie clearly had other ideas, as she was already headed for the sheriff's relic of a vehicle that he'd been using all day. He'd already put in a request for another SUV from the county's collection of confiscated drug transport vehicles. Most of those came with some cosmetic damage, but anything over five years old was sold at auction, anyway. The county bureaucrats took the best of the pool, but he'd settle for a late model four-wheel drive with some decent clearance. Winter around here could be hostile, just like his current mood.

"Allie, you don't get to walk away from me after pulling a stunt like that."

"I'm not walking away from anyone. I'm baiting the hook." Allie didn't say another word until she reached the passenger side of the car. She'd even lifted the handle without waiting for him to open her door, most likely to prove a point. Well, he'd heard her loud and clear. The thing of it was, he sure as hell didn't have to like it. "You asked me here to help you, Ken, and that's exactly what I'm going to do."

"You must be Allie." The blonde bartender set a club soda with a slice of lime on the counter with a smile. She'd just wiped her hands on a towel after cutting some fruit and sorting it into separate covered garnish bins. She offered a clean hand in reception. "I'm Brynn Mercer, owner of The Cavern and Lance Kendall's better half."

She returned Brynn's smile and shook the bartender's hand. Allie had already known the identity of the petite blonde. The woman had lost her parents at a young age and was taken in by a couple named Tiny and Rose Phifer, the former proprietors of The Cavern. They had all but raised Brynn through her teenage years and helped fund her business degree after graduation from the local high school.

So, why hadn't the serial killer targeted such a perfect victim?

It was one of the reasons Allie had chosen to make her way to the quaint bar while Mitch had to drive up to the lake to separate two locals before they came to blows over property rights and exactly whose dock was being searched by who.

After leaving his place and being on the receiving end of a *get your head out of your ass* lecture she hadn't experienced since her first year in the Corps, he'd finally taken the time to show her around the rest of the town. They'd even driven up to the lake and back, although both of them made sure there wasn't an unexpected run-in with Agent Thorne or his other agents while they were up there together.

Allie was uniquely aware of her boundaries on this case, and she would respect the decisions handed down by the chain of command. She was in Blyth Lake for nothing more than comforting an old friend who just happened to be the sheriff.

Technically, she could have ordered an alcoholic beverage seeing as she was on vacation…but she never drank when she carried. The chances of anyone catching her walking anywhere around this town without a fully loaded firearm was zero to none. Her badge and gun would always be within arm's reach.

"Everyone seems to know my name before I introduce my-self around here," Allie replied, noticing an older man who at first glance didn't appear to be in such good health. He'd been staring at her from one of the corner stools of the bar, and she'd recognized him instantly. He'd been the one to hold the door open for her at the diner this morning. She'd bet money that he was the infamous Cavern regular noted in the case file as one Jeremy Bell. "I'm just passing the time while Mitch finishes up some work on a domestic call."

"I heard the feds are still up at the lake searching all the private docks, boat houses, as well as both the boat yards. How they managed to secure a warrant that broad is beyond me,"

Miles Schaeffer said gruffly as he claimed a stool to Allie's left. He'd been at the diner this morning, too, having an in-depth conversation with the waitress about his older son who'd been arrested for attempted arson. It didn't take a very special federal agent or trained FBI profiler to figure out the man's identity. "I watch "Criminal Minds" and "NCIS" every week. I know how things work up there in the city."

Allie hid her smile behind the rim of her glass. She understood better than most that television programs weren't that accurate when it came to police investigations and procedures. But damn, if this place wasn't like the TV show "Cheers". She was expecting Norm to come rolling out any minute.

Miles Schaeffer didn't even bother telling Brynn his order. A cold draft beer was set in front of him before he'd even had a chance to get comfortable on the stool she suspected was his regular perch.

"Have you spoken with either Tiny or Rose today?" Jeremy asked, his gaze intermittently landing on Allie as if he were holding an inner debate on whether or not she should be included in his conversation. She wisely remained quiet, having learned long ago that listening resulted in more answers than any questions she could manage. "I'm sure this isn't good for anyone's business."

"Well, the restaurant and marina closed for the season right after Labor Day. They have a couple of cottages with docks rented out for the late Muskie fishing season, but the other cabins are still being renovated for next year." Brynn's gaze flickered toward the front entrance when it was pushed open to let the late afternoon sun shine through the doors. A glance in the mirror revealed none other than Jack Stuart. "Everyone is being very cooperative, so the search is going seamlessly from my understanding."

Not everyone, but that piece of news had yet to make the rounds.

Allie didn't have to look at her watch to know that it was a little after seventeen hundred hours. It was one of the reasons she'd decided to stop by The Cavern. The regulars would be getting off work right about now, and there was nothing more useful than listening to the gossip of the day at places like these, where the locals came to rant and decompress.

The entrance opened once more. This time, the crew was a little rowdier than the last.

"Brynn, could we get some longnecks with shots?" a man called out as he and some of his friends kept walking toward the taller tables located near the dartboards. "Just put the first round on my tab."

Miles muttered something under his breath about some people being entitled dipshits, but Allie could have easily mistaken the incoherent words. He pulled his beer closer as he gave her a sideways glance.

"Are you that special fed from Quantico? The one who's friends with Mitch?"

"I am," Allie replied with a nod. "I'm just passing the time until he gets back from up at the lake."

"It's not like there's much else to do here in town." Miles snorted as he exchanged knowing glances with Jeremy. "Although we do have a small theater that shows two different movies a night. The first showing is mostly for the families, cartoons and such. The R-rated movies don't usually come on until after dark. You know, with kids not being allowed and all."

"I like small towns like this," Allie said, beginning to lay the groundwork that would hopefully lead to an arrest. "I would have loved growing up here in Blyth Lake. It's really quite lovely. Having been raised in the city where I had to watch my back with every step I took wasn't the most pleasant childhood, if you know what I mean."

"See?" Miles said to Jeremy, having momentarily lost Allie with his arbitrary reply. His response wasn't what she'd been looking for, but it somehow landed her exactly where she'd wanted to steer the discussion. "That's what Clayton and Wes get for thinking the grass is greener on the other side. City life ain't all it's cracked up to be."

"I heard Wes was coming back into the fold," a rather nice-looking man said, sidling up to Allie. She didn't miss the fact that he was trying nonchalantly to look her over in the mirror. He was the one from earlier who apparently kept a tab open for him and his friends. "It's about time. Not everyone can make a go of it in the city."

"Billy," Miles greeted, though it was evident that he had a dislike for the younger man. "Is it true that your parents are buying up property all around the lake?"

Allie caught onto two things at once.

It was always a nice feeling to hit pay dirt in the first pan.

The man standing next to her elbow had to be none other than Billy Stanton. He was basically a trust fund baby, though he was currently working as a paramedic after flunking out of med school. He'd had to save face with the family name by demonstrating his civic spirit while finding a way to keep the lineage confined to the medical field. She suspected that he'd be in the running for mayor sometime in the next twenty years.

William Theodore Stanton, Jr. didn't fit the profile she'd created—at least, at face value. What Billy's past didn't reveal in writing was that his father had never been home to fulfill his fatherly duties, virtually making the household a single parent mansion devoid of supervision.

Billy was about the right age, had the right overall background, and pretty much checked the rest of the boxes she'd formed when constructing her profile with the exception of his current relationship with Julie Brigham.

Wasn't there always a stinger in the mix?

"Where did you hear that doozy?" Billy asked warily, his attention now solely focused on Miles. "From Noah Kendall? I was initially interested in his place because of the land. As for whatever real estate my father dabbles in, that's none of my concern."

Allie mulled over the insight Miles had just provided, wondering if his inquiry had any merit. She purposefully remained quiet, noticing that Brynn was doing the same. Now that woman had to be a wealth of information that Mitch had already tapped when it came to what was going on around town. There had to be things she'd overheard that she probably hadn't fully connected yet.

Brynn would be worthy of a private interview.

"I'm not sure where I heard that tidbit of information from exactly." Miles' eyes were slightly squinted as he continued to regard Billy with suspicion. "But I don't have to tell you that Tiny and Rose would never sell their lake property to anyone, no matter what they're offered."

"As I said, my parents don't keep me apprised of every real estate decision they are considering," Billy replied rather briskly, clearly attempting to end the conversation. It did leave one curious, though. Allie had dealt with many investigations where the parents did their best to cover up their children's crimes. If the Stantons were buying up private lake property around the unsub's former killing ground, did that mean they were in possession of information regarding their son's guilt or innocence? "Brynn, could we get a few orders of wings for the table? Have the cook drown and burn them."

There was no *please* or *thank you*. So much for small town manners. Allie was now rethinking that run at mayor. It was easy to see why Miles believed that Billy felt entitled, especially given his propensity to treat others with such contempt.

"You must be the friend Mitch invited to town," Billy said with a charming smile, channeling all his attention on her. His ability to alter his mood like flicking a switch was another telltale sign that he could be a sociopath and the possible suspect Mitch had been looking for in this investigation. She'd been hoping to stay under the radar and just listen to their exchange. Unfortunately, from her understanding, that didn't often happen in small towns. "I'm Billy Stanton."

"Allie Delaney," she replied, returning his loose, halfhearted handshake. She noticed right away that he was right-handed. "It's nice to meet you."

"You're from D.C., aren't you?" Billy nodded his thanks toward Brynn when she slid another bottle of beer his way. She'd put together a tray of four additional beers and five shots of what could only be whiskey to take over to the table he and his friends had claimed upon entering the establishment. "This must be quite the change for a city girl like you. No Starbucks for miles."

He just had to remind her of that inconvenience, hadn't he? No wonder people didn't like the man.

"I was just telling Mr. Schaeffer that I would have loved to have grown up in a town like this. Big cities are a lot rougher than you might think, even with a Starbucks on every corner." Allie didn't doubt that every word she uttered in this bar would be whispered in everyone's ears come morning. "Blyth Lake reminds me of a Norman Rockwell painting. I love it."

"Yeah, if you add splashes of red to those paintings," Billy said with a laugh that wasn't returned. He looked at everyone in the vicinity with disbelief. "Get it? Red for blood. Come on. We have a serial killer on the loose, snatching up all the available talent. You don't find that funny?"

"Jeremy is sitting at the end of the bar, in case you didn't notice. You need to keep talk like that to yourself," Brynn informed him in a low tone as she leaned over the bar. She'd yet to take the tray of beers and shots over to his table. "Your joke wasn't funny at all, Billy."

Jeremy Bell was the father of Whitney Bell, one of the serial killer's latest victims. Her murder had been the most recent, but long overdue in the psychopath's twisted perception of reality. It was easy to see his contempt for the younger man who had the compassion and common sense of a third-grader, and that was probably being overly generous.

"You're the one who went to medical school, aren't you?" Allie asked, turning her head so that Billy didn't miss her warning. "I can see the reason you didn't make it through the vetting process. Your bedside manner leaves a lot to be desired."

In the city, everyone had an opinion. It wasn't all that unusual, and it certainly didn't warrant gaining the attention of every individual within hearing distance. Blyth Lake was different, and Allie had known better than to draw additional, unwanted attention, more so than she already had. The bar had become excruciatingly silent, allowing the music from the jukebox to suddenly be front and center.

Damn it.

It was obvious that Billy didn't have a whole lot of people call him out, because he was still standing next to her with a slack-jawed incredulous expression. She didn't break eye contact with him until he did in their one-sided dual of wills.

"I like her, Jeremy," Miles said, breaking the tension as he lifted his beer in salute. "Welcome to Blyth Lake, Allie."

Allie was relatively sure she heard the usual *fuck you* exclamation muttered underneath Billy's breath before he turned on the heel of his expensive brown loafers. A medic certainly couldn't afford Italian designer hand-tooled leather shoes or the expensive name brand clothes he was wearing, which left her to believe he did live off that trust fund his parents had set up for him. It was most likely one that he never had to worry about running short on funds.

"I like you, too," Brynn replied with a wide smile. "You'll fit in around here just fine."

Brynn lifted the tray of longneck beers and top shelf whiskies before exiting from her spot behind the bar. She was more than happy to drown Billy's self-inflicted wounds in mildly expensive alcohol.

Allie wasn't sure why the woman would say something about her fitting in, especially considering that this visit was temporary. Mitch *had* explained her reasons for being here to his immediate family, hadn't he?

"Mr. Bell, I heard about your daughter," Allie said softly, trying to undo some of the unpleasantness Billy Stanton had spewed out. "You have my deepest condolences, sir."

Jeremy stared back at her with an intensity that would have made most people uncomfortable. He still wasn't sure of her character, and she couldn't blame him for using a discerning manner. There were a lot of strangers milling about Blyth Lake due to the news coverage of the serial killer, and they all wanted to cash in by singling out something about the case...more likely a story that would make their name national news.

"Molly mentioned that you're a profiler for the FBI." Jeremy turned the coffee mug on the old wooden surface of the bar over and over as he weighed his thoughts. It had been detailed in Whitney's report that her father was an unrepentant alcoholic.

Had the tragedy of losing his daughter changed his ways? It wasn't unheard of in cases like this. "Is that true?"

"Yes, although I'm not here in any official capacity." Allie didn't want to get anyone's hopes up that she could contribute to the investigation in any meaningful way. She wasn't a miracle worker, though she did believe she could draw the unsub out into the open. Her background was exactly what he looked for in a victim…a female with an unhappy childhood. "I'm a friend of Mitch's from way back. But if I can provide any insight into the case, I won't hesitate to do so."

Jeremy nodded slowly, all the while never breaking eye contact.

"What do you make of those letters the killer is sending Charlene Winston?" Miles asked after taking a swig of his beer. He was totally oblivious to the silent conversation hanging in the air between Allie and Jeremy. "You'd think there was a way to get fingerprints off the paper, like they do in those crime shows. Maybe even sweat DNA."

Allie didn't let on that the letters being sent to the reporter were being done so over an anonymous message app that hid the user of the blind account by not requiring the sender to enter his own email address.

Agent Thorne was currently attempting to get a warrant for the company who created the app in order to have them hand over any information they might have, including IP connections, but privacy laws were shielding them from that legal action. In the meantime, Jay and his team would have to continue their search and hope that positive DNA results came back from the bullet Gwen Kendall discharged from her weapon.

Recalling that the unsub would most likely be favoring his left arm in some manner, Allie glanced over her shoulder to the group of men surrounding one of the two dartboards. Billy

Stanton was still holding his bottle of beer with his right hand. He hadn't done anything with his left side to give any indication he had a wound on the outer part of his left shoulder or upper arm.

Allie turned back so that she had full view of the mirror in front of her, searching out Jack Stuart. She wasn't surprised to find that he made no attempt to hide the fact that he was staring directly at her. There wasn't a suspect that she couldn't stare down, and she sure as hell didn't want Jack Stuart to believe that he had the upper hand just because he was an odd character. She had no doubt that she could wipe the floor with him in a close combat situation.

"Speak of the devil," Miles muttered, waving his hand at Brynn as she made her way back behind the bar. Allie waited until Jack finally broke eye contact, glancing toward Brynn. He must have been curious as to what Miles was talking about, which meant he'd heard every word she'd said since his arrival. Good. That's exactly what she'd wanted. "Brynn, turn up the volume. There's that reporter again."

Sure enough, the redheaded reporter appeared solemn as the camera focused on her pretty congenial face. On one hand, the impromptu broadcast prevented Allie from having to answer Miles Schaeffer about fingerprints or sweat DNA on some paper that didn't even exist.

Unfortunately, such an interruption couldn't be good news.

Concern immediately spread among the patrons of the bar as Brynn reached for the remote that had been stored underneath the bar for everyone's protection. It wasn't long before everyone had gathered around the outer line of stools to hear the latest announcement.

"...coming to you again from Blyth Lake, Ohio with an update on the Blyth Lake Serial Killer." Charlene Winston was a professional, and she knew exactly when to insert a long pause for effect. "It's come to our attention that the FBI has brought a person of interest into the local police station for formal questioning. We are live on the scene. There are no details as of yet, but we will remain vigilant in our duties to…"

"Well, I'll be damned," Miles muttered, his frown immediately turning into a big wide grin. "Jeremy, this could be it. This nightmare could finally over."

Allie truly wished that she could join in the celebration, but she understood all too well that nothing was ever written in stone and the recent news report said nothing of any real value. Who had Jay brought in for questioning? Was he or she a material witness or a suspect? If the latter, on what grounds?

There were too many unanswered questions to revel in the relief these people desired. She also couldn't help but casually set her gaze on Billy Stanton's reflection only to find that he wasn't looking at the television screen like the rest of the clientele…he was staring directly back at her using the same exact mirror.

CHAPTER SEVEN

MITCH WAS ONCE again running on next to no sleep, but that didn't keep him from taking two cups of coffee out to the front porch. The snap of the screen door closing behind him didn't prevent the crickets from exchanging their love songs for more than a brief moment.

One of the many saving graces about this time of year was that the mosquitos were no longer out in full force. Quite often during the summer, one had to virtually dip oneself in bug spray to avoid being eaten alive.

Mitch's dad always fogged his yard and made sure to treat any standing body of water on his property for the little flying menaces, but not everyone was so conscientious. Fall temperatures rendered those precautions obsolete, allowing everyone to enjoy bonfires and sitting out on the porch without all that mess. One just needed to wear warm clothing.

The fact that Allie Delaney was sitting on his porch swing was an added bonus to the season.

He'd made that initial phone call to her for assistance in the investigation, but he'd never imagined in a million years that she would purposefully put herself in harm's way to attract the attention of the killer. All he'd wanted was her help to unlock the secrets of whatever darkness had been hidden in Blyth Lake for over a decade.

Mitch refused to allow Allie to be swallowed by the shadows

that hid this demon from plain sight. He was sure once he had a bead on this animal, he would finish this one way or another.

Mitch had worked side by side with Allie for a number of years and had been her friend for much longer. Now that they were both out of the Marines, she wouldn't have as much trouble keeping up with his latest address.

He'd never once considered her background as being similar to those of the young girls who'd lost their lives. Allie had never used her unhappy childhood as a crutch, therefore it was easy to forget she'd been raised by an alcoholic father who spent more money on booze than he ever had on his daughter.

The moment Mitch forbid Allie from pursuing this dangerous game that she was playing and knowing that it could get her killed, he was certain that would all but guarantee that she'd run headlong into the raging flames of fire. She'd never admit it, but she was an adrenaline junkie addicted to the thrill of the hunt. He needed to manage this delicate situation just right, which meant sending her back to D.C. and losing the advantage of having her here.

"Do you need a heavier jacket than the blazer you have on?" Mitch asked, carefully handing over the steaming mug that included way too much sugar and cream to his liking. Hell, he took his coffee black. It was simpler that way. "And when did you switch from black coffee to this shit?"

Dusk had fallen, but the porch light cast enough illumination that he had no trouble making out Allie's striking features. Her chestnut hair was still pulled back in a knot, and a loose silky portion framed her heart-shaped face. He remembered tucking that same strand of hair behind her ear the one night they…

Mitch caught himself before allowing his thoughts to stray too far.

He didn't regret a single second of that night they'd been

intimate together, but he'd also known that they led two distinctly different lives for anything more than that to develop between them. There also hadn't been enough time for it to grow into something more.

They'd made the right decision to keep their relationship confined to just being friends.

Why, then, was reversing his decision to have her come here so damned hard to say?

"There's an exceptional café or Starbucks practically on every corner in D.C." Allie had somehow managed to curl her legs underneath her on the padded porch swing, regardless that she had on a pair of brown leather knee-high boots. She smiled up at him when he remained standing. "After a while, black coffee just didn't cut it. I got used to living in civilization, and I adjusted to the availability of condiments."

He figured she was referring to the late nights of numerous investigations, the long hours sweating over a profile that could make or break a case, and making endless adjustments as each gruesome murder or violent act took place.

He didn't envy her schedule, and he sure as hell didn't picture himself having to deal with the same shit here in such a small town with a population of around twenty-three hundred residents. He certainly hadn't expected that poison to take root in his hometown.

"Shelby Tilmadge is on a forty-eight hour hold at University Hospitals of Cleveland until a psych evaluation can be ordered," Mitch shared with her, having just gotten off the phone with Agent Thorne. It was better to start slow and work up to what he needed to happen. "We all know Shelby couldn't hurt a flea, but his detailed confession about the murders was enough for the prosecutor to take notice of him. No charges have been pressed, but it's going to be a shitstorm when the public realizes that Shelby is just a disturbed individual who confessed to several murders all because he believes those damned aliens and their mothership can't reach him behind bars."

"I bet Jay is fit to be tied." Allie lifted her lashes to reveal her brown eyes, both darker in this light than he was used to seeing. He could physically see the change in her body language when she concentrated solely on business. "Did Special Agent Theo Stringer provide you with the updated profile?"

"No, not yet. If he's given it to Agent Thorne, I don't know anything about it." Mitch didn't have to say another word for her to know of his displeasure at the fact that Stringer had other *priorities*. If that was the case, then the FBI needed to find the funding to employ more agents with a background in behavioral sciences. "Speaking of which, you never gave me the profile you worked up."

In those few phone conversations Mitch did have with Allie, she'd expressed that her way of doing things was completely opposite of how Stringer wrote up a profile. Stringer would rather take what was on paper and create an outline of an individual. Allie had always worked better in the field where she could sense the environment, catching things that could alter the slightest detail of her report based on local changes in lifestyle and family customs.

Small Town, America was entirely different than what one might find in the larger cities. People continued customs their ancestors kept from their origins, local people shared common schooling, and people knew each other intimately as a matter of everyday proximity.

"You've been a bit busy," Allie reminded him with a lift of her pink lips. She must have applied a fresh coat of lip gloss after dinner, which unfortunately hadn't included his father or the rest of the family. Mitch had no choice but to postpone their family gathering due to the media circus outside the station. He was beginning to think the cancellation wasn't such a bad idea, considering his siblings were already making Allie's visit out to be more than what it truly was meant to be. "At least we know why Patty didn't answer Jack Stuart's phone call today."

Mitch took comfort in knowing that the lines to the sheriff's office switched over to the 911 state facilities should a real emergency have taken place. Shelby Tilmadge usually didn't qualify as much more than a nuisance, though that had changed quickly once he started spouting on about chains and borrowing boats to take his victims out to the middle of the lake to sink their remains. Patty had already been made aware of the situation and had been fielding numerous calls from the residents coming and going over the county line.

Mitch debated joining Allie on the porch swing, but he thought better of it. He needed to utilize this private time with her to gain insight into her thoughts and views on how to capture the individual they were all looking for. After that, he needed her far away from here.

"I didn't bring you here to act as bait to draw out a serial killer, Allie." Mitch purposefully chose the seat that faced the property. It allowed him to still make out her expressions while also giving him an overview of the approach up the driveway. He instinctively tensed at the excitement that flashed in her eyes that were no longer dark. "What you've been doing is dangerous, and it sure as hell wasn't the reason I asked you here."

So much for subtlety.

"What I did was plant a few seeds in the right soil," Allie corrected him quietly, resting the mug on the side of her knee as it was clear she was choosing her words carefully. "You have to admit it's a brilliant plan, Ken. Everyone in a small town like this talks. It will spread like a wildfire."

"It's also a contingency that Agent Thorne and I didn't sign off on. He doesn't even want you here, let alone being stalked out like some sacrificial lamb. Hell, the Bureau would probably kick your ass to the curb if they realized you were in Blyth Lake doing what you've been doing all day."

Mitch ran a hand over his face, wishing he could crawl into bed for the next twelve hours. Hell, he wouldn't even be opposed to having her by his side if he thought they could survive the same arrangement as last time.

That boat had sailed long ago, and he was at a stage of his life where he needed to find himself a home along with every-thing that came with that moniker. Being a civilian had initially put him into a tailspin, and he wouldn't be able to recover until the ground appeared below him and he could see his way clear of this mess.

Even then, he wasn't sure he was cut out for the type of relationship Allie would want. He wasn't blind or deaf. She'd said on more than one occasion herself that she wasn't cut out for a life of commitment.

Mitch didn't doubt that it was because of her childhood, but they'd never delved that deep into their subconscious with one another. Not even the night they'd slept together. Hell, they'd both been drinking and knew better.

"How am I supposed to explain your agenda to Thorne once he hears what you've done?"

Allie shrugged, clearly not worried about her colleague or his response to her behavior.

"Look, the profile that Stringer put together is pretty damned accurate. I wouldn't change it much, with the exception of what I amended this morning. With that said, being here in this town changes things by virtue of what and who these people are." Allie tapped her finger on the handle of the mug, as if she were doing her best to select the right words. "You know the unsub, Mitch. For all we know, he's probably been to your father's house for dinner. We've already established that, but he is someone you grew up with…someone from your generation. When his identity is eventually revealed, you'll find that he's said or done things that should have tipped you off long ago. This isn't the type of unsub where the neighbors are questioning how this could have happened, all because he was a genuinely nice guy who helped a neighbor unload her groceries from her car and she forgot to say thank you."

"You're saying that we *are* looking at someone like Shelby Tilmadge, who has been right in front of us the whole time."

"No. Shelby has delusions about being abducted and probed by aliens." Allie unfolded her legs and gently set the soles of her boots on the wooden planks of the old porch. She leaned forward as she became engrossed in the topic of conversation, seemingly wanting him to feel the same sense of urgency. He ignored the fact that the light fragrance of her perfume consumed the scent of autumn. "The unsub you're looking for is an everyday average Joe, but he's been vocal about his loneliness and appears very unassuming."

"Do you believe he's an only child?"

"Originally, I would have said yes." Allie slowly shook her head, as if there was something just out of reach that she couldn't touch. "There's something about the young girls…sisters…that has the unsub's attention. Why not target young men? If he wants a complete family, why only young girls reaching that tender age where they are just beginning their lives as women?"

"Have you seen the stock of teenage boys around here? They're taller, wider, and stronger than the average male was at our age." Mitch didn't think it too odd that young women were targeted versus young males. "Are you saying there's something more to that?"

"Maybe." Allie leaned back against the porch swing, using her boots to create a slow sway. "I was at The Cavern when you were dealing with Shelby and that entire media circus you had to manage. Jack Stuart walked in, but I also had the unique pleasure of meeting Billy Stanton and his band of merry misfits."

Mitch had been about to take a drink of his coffee, but the way she'd verbalized Billy's name had him changing his mind. The Stantons were wealthy, and Billy had always believed he was untouchable. Outside the law. But just because the man was a complete asshole didn't mean that he was capable of cold-blooded murder.

"I didn't get a chance to see if Stanton was favoring his left arm, but I do recall Jack Stuart giving us a glimpse of the slightest wince when he rested his left elbow on the window of his truck." Allie gave another small shrug as she continued to mull over the details of the case. "Jack is an only child, and he fits the rest of the profile. Then again, so do a lot of men in this lovely town."

Mitch had noticed Jack's earlier reaction as well, but almost every male in Blyth Lake worked some type of manual trade job. Injuries were common. This small town wasn't a city that catered to white collar jobs, with the exception of business owners. In reality, it wouldn't be hard to whittle down the suspect list with a simple slap on the arm.

Maybe he should arrange an arm wrestling contest at the Cavern. The local men would line up for something like that with bragging rights attached. Anyone opting out of a chance to prove his bravado would stand out in the crowd. *Hmmm.* Maybe a darts tournament would suffice.

"Billy was raised in a wealthy family with both parents."

Mitch was relying on the profiles he'd been given by both Stringer and Allie, but that didn't mean he was putting all his eggs in one basket. Also, Allie had brought up Stanton for a reason. "He doesn't fit your profile."

"He has two parents, but that doesn't mean he was raised by both. Lack of supervision might be enough," Allie pointed out, lifting the coffee cup to her pink lips. She slowed the swing with her boot so she could take another sip. Mitch honestly liked having her here to bounce ideas off of, but it was coming time to tell her the truth—she needed to be far away from here after the stunt she'd pulled today. "He's a likely suspect, and one you should check out. There's something else that Stringer will probably add to his profile."

"And what would that be?"

Mitch was glad he'd steeled himself against her answer, because it almost sounded as if a war had been declared on the town. Then again, hadn't he already known that?

"Questioning Shelby would have given relief to many serial killers who don't like the attention. That's not so with the unsub you're looking for." Allie inhaled deeply before explaining in detail what that could mean for Mitch, Agent Thorne, and the other law enforcement men and women working this case. "These residents whom the unsub feels protective over has—"

"Protective?" Mitch couldn't help but interrupt Allie's insightful lecture. There was no way in hell that son of a bitch felt *protective* over this town or its people. He'd killed young girls in cold blood, the same teenagers the unsub had grown up with, if the profile was even somewhat close to being right. "He tore families apart, and by your accounts this bastard stood back and looked on as this town has grieved over and over again for the past decade."

"The unsub believes that he's saving those girls by giving

them a family they never had. Don't think I'm defending this monster by any means. I'm not. But if you're going to catch him, you must get in his head to read his thoughts and motives." Allie gave Mitch a sympathetic smile for what he and his constituents were going through. They'd always been comrades, and he didn't appreciate her looking at him as if he were on the losing end. "Have you noticed the letters getting more frequent or the way he went from addressing Charlene Winston in a proper manner to using her first name now that he's come to know her? His letters are revealing more and more about his past, because he *wants* the residents of Blyth Lake to understand who he is and what he's worked so hard to accomplish."

"He loves the attention, because it makes him feel as if he's part of society." Mitch recognized the path Allie had taken, and it was as if a boulder had been set upon his shoulders. The weight was almost unbearable. "Now all the attention is on Shelby, not the unsub."

Allie slowly nodded, almost as if she were wishing she could give him better news. Unfortunately, there was nothing good about this scenario. She was all but warning him that something bad was headed their way just when he didn't think things could get any worse.

"The unsub wants his sense of family back, Ken. The attention on his letters gave him a familial awareness, but now that's been taken from him, too." Allie tilted her head as she hammered another nail in the proverbial coffin. "There is no doubt in my mind that the unsub will start hunting again, and very soon."

CHAPTER EIGHT

THE CLANGING SOUND of metal pots and pans reverberated through Allie and irritated every nerve in her body. She rolled a little more into the soft pillow and buried her face in the cool cotton, wishing more than anything that godawful noise would stop.

It didn't.

She groaned as she rolled over onto the most comfortable mattress that she'd ever had the pleasure of sleeping on, fully expecting the sun to be shining through the windows. All she could see once she'd forced her lashes open was a grayish cast slipping through the slats in the wooden blinds.

Weren't the blinds at her B&B made of vinyl?

Allie sat straight up in bed, now fully awake. She slowly took in her surroundings, noting the knotted oak bedposts, burgundy and brown colors mixed together on the warm comforter, and the fact that there was a man's robe hanging on the adjacent bathroom door.

"Damn it," Allie muttered, tossing the comforter and covers aside.

She must have fallen asleep on Mitch's couch last night when they'd retired to the living room after the night air became too chilly. The last thing she remembered was him taking a phone call from Agent Thorne about Shelby Tilmadge's psych evaluation. She'd only meant to close her eyes for a second.

Having taken the redeye in the night before, she'd been running on practically no sleep.

The only good thing to have come out of her sleep-induced coma was the fact that she'd gotten out of yet another lecture. Mitch hadn't fooled her in the least with the conversation they'd had on the porch. He was all but gearing up to send her packing.

A quick glance down showed her that Mitch had left her in jeans and the tank top she'd been wearing underneath her turtleneck and insulated blazer. A moment of panic enveloped her as she hastily put her hand to her hip, searching for her firearm. It was then she saw her weapon in its clip-on style holster carefully set on the nightstand atop her leather-bound credentials.

As she swung her legs over the side of the bed to reach for her firearm, she noticed that he'd also removed her socks. Had he done so without thinking or did he remember she couldn't sleep with her toes confined? It was an old argument they had once debated about keeping one's boots on while getting rest in a combat zone.

Upon some reflection, it was better not to know the answer to that question.

They'd only been intimate once.

It wasn't likely to happen again.

Allie secured her weapon to her side and then made quick use of the bathroom, even taking the time to use her finger as a makeshift toothbrush. The minty taste would suffice until she was able to make it back to her room at the B&B. There was no sign of her blazer, socks, or boots in the bedroom, which meant he'd taken them off of her in the living room.

How Mitch had managed to achieve that task without waking her was nothing short of a miracle.

There was a part of her that wished she'd been aware of

every single stroke of his hand, but the rational part of her brain screamed back that it had saved her from a complication far too complex for her to field at this point in her life.

She quietly opened the bedroom door, still wanting a few moments to gather her composure. The hairband that she'd had in last night had come out, but she hadn't been able to locate it in the bed. It was probably with her stuff downstairs, but not having her hair pulled back was like not having her vest on during a felony arrest.

Allie rested her hand on the wooden railing and slid it downward with each step of the staircase. The hardwood floor wasn't as cold on her bare feet as she would have thought, and she wondered if he'd turned the heat on last night. There had been a report on the radio about the temperature falling into the mid-forties during the early morning hours.

The delicious smell of bacon permeated the air, but it couldn't hide the rich aroma of fresh ground coffee being made. It wasn't espresso, but it was good enough. She inhaled deeply while soundlessly searching for the rest of her clothes.

The living room was spotless.

She contemplated going back upstairs to see if she'd missed them laying out on a chair somewhere, but her stomach grumbled and her mouth salivated at the whiffs of breakfast.

The best course of action was to make light of the fact that she'd fallen asleep, so her words were already on the tip of her tongue as she stepped through the doorway and into the kitchen.

"Do you always undress unconscious women and put them in your bed, Ken? With your looks, I would have thought—"

Fuck.

Double fuck.

Allie came up short, wishing a gigantic hole would open up in the ceramic tile underneath her feet and swallow her whole.

Mitch wasn't the one standing at the stove with a red and white checkerboard apron tied around his neck and waist. A stranger with a toothpick tucked in one side of his mouth had turned at the sound of her entrance. He was holding a spatula in one hand and a cup of coffee in the other. A familiar smile graced his lips, and his blue eyes sparkled with a hint of mischief.

The man standing before her could only be Gus Kendall.

Allie's words echoed back to her, and she tried to retract her statement.

"I wasn't unconscious, sir. I mean, I'd fallen asleep, but I wasn't completely incoherent." The wider Gus Kendall's smile became, the more she realized what a mess she was making out of this impromptu run-in. She was going to kill Mitch. "What I'm trying to say is that Ken treated me with the upmost respect, like the gentleman you raised him to be. Mitch. I mean, Mitch. Your son did nothing wrong and—"

"Allie, meet my father," Mitch murmured from behind her, having appeared from out of nowhere. She was too mortified to even care that he'd scared the shit out of her. Technically, her brain had short-circuited the moment his warm hands had encased her upper arms from behind. "Dad, this is Allie Delaney. Did you manage to finally get some sleep?"

Allie cleared her throat, moving to the side faster than she thought possible without having the added help of caffeine. She shot Mitch a look that told him sleep hadn't been the issue.

As a matter of fact, she wished more than anything she could go back upstairs and get out on the other side of the bed. Maybe then this day wouldn't have started off with her being completely mortified at meeting Mitch's father for the first time.

"It's nice to meet you, Mr. Kendall," Allie managed to say after Mitch had given her a bit of space. She'd even wiped her perspiring palm against her jeans before walking across the kitchen floor and shaking his hand. "I'm sorry about all that from before. I thought Mitch was in here or else I never would have—"

"Oh, please," Gus laughed, gesturing with his spatula that she should have a seat. "Call me Gus. I've heard a lot about you, Allie. When Mitch here called me this morning and told me that he couldn't make it to the diner for breakfast, I decided to bring breakfast to him. He told me that the two of you were working on the case most of last night and decided not to drive back into town so late. I don't blame you for staying out here one bit. The B&B is nice enough, but I've heard Florence's sheets can be a bit scratchy. So, what will it be? Eggs, French toast, or a breakfast steak?"

Allie didn't have to look to her right to know that Mitch had taken a seat at the kitchen table rather than trying to help prepare the meal. Seeing as this was an older farmhouse, the kitchen didn't have an island like the more modern ones today. Even the stove was one of those natural gas ones with the open burners, although it looked to be a newer model. The place had a homey feel that she couldn't quite equate with the Mitch she knew, but then again…he wasn't the same man she'd had in her bed for an overnight a year ago.

"I haven't had French toast in years," Allie admitted, her nerves having settled a bit after such a rough start. She ran a hand through her hair, still wishing she had the hairband to secure the messy strands at the base of her neck. "I'd love some, thank you."

"Coming right up," Gus announced, turning back to the stove and allowing her to finally shoot Mitch a look that hopefully contained many sharp pointed daggers. He was hiding that rare smile of his behind his coffee mug. Oh, he thought this was funny, did he? "So, Allie. Mitch was catching me up on last night's event with Shelby Tilmadge and his lunacy. I didn't believe for a second that he was the one committing all those murders. He's actually more timid than his father."

"Have there been any new developments?" Allie asked, skimming her gaze over the counter and finding that beautiful machine that promised the nectar of the gods. It didn't take her long to fetch herself a cup of coffee, and she didn't even have to go looking for cream and sugar. Gus or Mitch had already placed both commodities in the middle of the table. "I know you spoke with Jay last night."

Allie didn't tack on that Mitch's conversation with her fellow colleague was the last thing she remembered, but he was a smart enough guy to have gotten her cue.

"As we thought, Shelby had no real inside information about the crime scenes or any of the investigation's confidential details." Mitch slid the bowl of sugar her way as he continued to fill her in on the case. He shouldn't get to look so damned good when her appearance was so disheveled. "I believe an announcement is forthcoming, which is bound to create another media circus after they realize Shelby was nothing more than a distraction."

Allie figured that was going to happen anyway, because this unsub would have reacted without being too circumspect after Shelby was brought in for questioning. The media had all but made it sound as if an arrest of a prime suspect was imminent. She was honestly surprised to find that Mitch hadn't received a phone call with grisly news of another body or some young gal gone missing.

It struck her that she might have missed her chance last night to catch the unsub. Had he come looking for her at the B&B after she'd practically laid down a trail of neon signs? She pondered over that thought as she enjoyed her first cup of coffee and allowed the caffeine to seep into her system.

"What are your plans for the day?" Allie asked Mitch, figuring that she would head back to the B&B to shower and get cleaned up before mingling with the press and some of the residents who would no doubt be milling about town.

There were quite a few reporters who she'd love to listen in on without directly engaging, especially Charlene Winston. That woman had been living and breathing this investigation. Reporters could be a wealth of information, especially if they were chasing a lead they'd ferreted out on a nationwide story like theirs.

"I've got to head into the station. I have a meeting with Thorne before I have to check over the logs to make sure Blyth Lake is still the insane yet ordinary community I was hired to protect." Mitch cast a glance toward his father. "I was also hoping to stop by Gwen's office sometime this morning to see how she's healing up."

"Oh, I wouldn't do that. All you'll hear is Beth Ann go on and on about her wedding plans. Molly was telling everyone this morning that Jack asked Beth Ann to marry him last night in what was a fairly public proposal. Apparently, he took her up to the lake after a movie at the theater. The neighborhood groups up there are trying to pull everyone together in the face of what's happened. Jack popped the question in front of a whole crowd of their friends, and she said yes."

Had Allie judged Jack unfairly? He wasn't the most upstanding man in Blyth Lake, and he certainly had a wandering eye. That was proven within minutes of meeting him. But to take a massive leap into a proposal of marriage wasn't the reaction she believed the unsub would make to regain the town's attention.

Unless it was a way to bring a young girl into his makeshift home now that there was no longer a gravesite to secure his *sisters.*

"Here you go," Gus announced, startling Allie into sitting back when he set a plate in front of her that was piled high with...French toast pumpkins? "Happy Halloween, Allie. Now eat those up. There's more if you have room for them. After you're done with breakfast, I was hoping you'd join me in town today to pick out a selection of candy to hand out to the kids tonight."

Join him in picking out candy?

Allie shot an accusing stare across the table at Mitch. Had he set this up? Did he believe that her spending time with his father was going to prevent her from doing what he'd asked her not to do last night?

He couldn't call in a favor and then decide to take it back. When she said he could tuck it away for another time, she'd said that to be nice. Technically, she'd done it for selfish reasons. She didn't want the last thread that kept them together to disintegrate.

But Mitch didn't get to sit her on the sidelines. Hell, she had close combat training just like him, along with additional self-defense training at the FBI Academy. She could damn well take care of herself.

"I was hoping to—"

Mitch stood abruptly from the table, all four feet of his chair scraping across the tiled floor. He made the pretense of reaching for the syrup to speak to her so that his father couldn't hear.

"Please don't hurt my father's feelings by brushing his offer aside," Mitch murmured, his warm breath caressing her ear and bringing back memories that had no place here.

"You were saying?" Gus asked, having gone back to the stove to turn off the gas underneath the skillet. He then began untying the apron strings around his neck, warily looking at

Mitch trying to discern if something was wrong. She'd already gotten off on a bad foot, and she certainly didn't want to sink both her bare feet into the mud. "Allie?"

"I was just hoping you wouldn't mind stopping by the B&B so that I could take a quick shower and grab a change of clothes," Allie replied with a smile, landing her attention squarely on Gus. She didn't want to see Mitch's reaction to her response. She'd accepted that she would meet his family, but she'd never put it in context before. She reminded herself once again that they were only friends, and his father's friendship was only an extension of that relationship. "It wasn't my intention to fall asleep on Mitch's couch."

Yes, she'd purposefully added on that last statement so that Gus Kendall didn't get the wrong idea. It was for her own peace of mind that she set the boundaries and stick to them. All of this could have been avoided if only she hadn't been so exhausted from lack of sleep due to the redeye.

"Of course." Gus gave her a wink as he leaned against the counter to finish the rest of his coffee. It was like seeing Mitch in thirty-some years. "I can check on that entryway table I made for Florence while we're there and maybe get another cup of—"

The ringing of Mitch's cell phone stopped Gus from saying another word. The call could have simply been from one of his brothers or sister. It could have been the dispatcher or one of his deputies reaching out because an ongoing neighborhood dispute over somebody's cat. After all, she'd heard that happened quite often in small towns like Blyth Lake.

Unfortunately, it was none of those reasons.

"I'll be right there," Mitch exclaimed, showing her a glimpse of the man she remembered from their time in the Corps. The gravity of his expression told them enough about the situation to put them both on edge, but what he said next told her she'd been right in the adjusted profile she'd explained to him last night. "Charlene Winston is missing. Her cameraman found a letter this morning…Thorne believes it to be from the killer."

CHAPTER NINE

"THERE'S REALLY NOT much else for you to do here, Sheriff. The forensic team is still sweeping the scene to bag and tag trace evidence for the lab," Agent Thorne said, stuffing his notepad into the interior pocket of his designer suit jacket. It took every ounce of restraint Mitch had not to yank that pad out of his jacket and rip every page of it into small pieces right in front of him. Hell, he'd been questioned and dismissed by Thorne just as the man had done to every other guest at the inn. Special Agent Jay Thorne had absolutely no interpersonal communication skills whatsoever. "My team and I have this covered."

Mitch curled his fingers into the palm of his hand, tightening his fist until he'd regained some of his composure. Thorne remained oblivious to his impending doom and carried on as usual. Main Street had practically come to a standstill with every shop owner standing across the street in a tight crowd. Every curious gaze was staring at the B&B as if the large house was going to grow arms and legs. At least, when they weren't answering the probing questions of the media onsite.

"Those reporters seem to have everything covered, too. Do you want to invite them in to go over the crime scene with you and your guys?" Mitch didn't bother to hide his disdain at how this investigation was being handled. "Thorne, every single decision you make today is going to be broadcast on the evening news. Patty already released the press statement you wrote up regarding Shelby being discounted as a viable suspect. All eyes are glued to how you feds and my department handle this latest abduction."

"I'm used to shit like this, Kendall. It's nothing new to me. Maybe you could move the rest of the reporters back across the street." Thorne slipped his hands inside the pockets of his pants, casually glancing across the road to study the onlookers. Mitch had already sent a text to Allie, asking her if the unsub was the type to personally visit his crime scenes after the fact. She'd replied with one word—*no*. If he read between the lines, which were basically nonexistent, she was telling him that the serial killer was too busy preparing his latest family member for internment in whatever new killing ground he'd found. "Special Agent Stringer sent over his adjusted profile this morning. I've left a copy of it on your desk, but I'm guessing that you don't need to read through it seeing as you have your own profiler close at hand."

Mitch remained silent about the fact that he'd personally brought in Allie on an investigation that she had no business being part of, recognizing Thorne's jab for what it was.

The question remained—would the unsub have targeted Allie instead of Charlene had Allie been in her room at the inn last night?

The paralyzingly obvious answer made him physically nauseous to think that he could have put her life in danger. He'd asked her here as a professional to profile a sick individual, not to make herself a target. He'd wanted a fresh set of eyes to look at what they'd all been staring at for weeks, but not at this cost.

It was time to send Allie packing.

"You and I both know that it will take another week for Stringer to add his insights about the events of what happened to Charlene Winston last night to the report." Mitch hated the bureaucracy of these types of investigations, but he'd rather deal with delayed paperwork than risk Allie's safety. "Regardless, these are still my people. I'm not leaving until you've cleared the scene and the townsfolk can go about their business."

"Have it your way, Kendall." Thorne looked over Mitch's shoulder. "Just don't make this another family reunion, alright?"

Mitch turned to find Noah, Lance, and Irish crossing the street. He met them halfway, heeding Thorne's warning about their interference. This was no place for family or friends to congregate, no matter how bad they wanted answers.

"Dad called us," Noah said, glancing back over Mitch's shoulder at the forensics team who was finishing up their work. "Why would the killer take Charlene Winston?"

"Because she came from a broken family just like the rest of them," Irish replied quietly, his dark eyes full of concern as he took in the scene before them.

Mitch regarded Irish a little more closely, wondering how he'd known that fact about a complete stranger none of them knew much about. Something else was going on here, and he'd hate for Irish to be on Thorne's radar. The town's mechanic had suffered enough already.

To say it had come as a complete surprise to everyone to learn that Irish's sister had been one of the victims was an understatement. It certainly gave him ammunition to want this son of a bitch captured and put down for good.

"You sound as if you're personally acquainted with Ms. Winston." Mitch recalled Lance saying something about Irish being interested in a woman from town, but he never imagined it would have been the reporter who had published such salacious headlines. Her actions had caused more headaches than providing anyone with actual usable information. Mitch had nothing personal against Charlene Winston, but he didn't appreciate how she'd been so eager to facilitate the killer's bidding by publishing those letters without first talking to either Mitch or the feds. "Is there something I should know?"

"We've been spending time together off the books, if that's what you're asking." Irish still hadn't taken his eyes off the porch where the letter had been discovered on the worn welcome mat. "I realize that Charlene has caused a few ripples in the community, but she wasn't related to those victims. The investigation called to her for several reasons, one of which was her career. She had to pull a lot of strings at her network so that she could remain the lead on this story."

"When was the last time you saw Charlene Winston?"

"Mitch, that's unfair," Lance interrupted, shaking his head in disappointment. "Irish is just friends with her, that's all."

"I didn't say I had a problem with his choice of friends." Mitch and his siblings had been raised to have loyalty, and he didn't expect Lance to act any other way. "I'd rather cover this ground so that Special Agent Thorne doesn't have to track you down and haul you in later, if you get my drift. He struggles making friends as it is."

"I haven't seen Charlene in a few days with all the excitement regarding Shelby Tilmadge," Irish responded, and Mitch got the sense that the unusually private man was telling the truth. He inhaled deeply, almost as if he'd made an internal decision. "I'm heading back to the garage. I'll touch base later to see if you need me to answer any more questions."

Mitch monitored Irish's progression through the gathered crowd. Thorne had probably seen the entire exchange, and he would most likely hear about Irish and Charlene's intimate relationship at some point from the gossip mill. This could very easily turn into a circus. Due to the close nature of their friendship, it made it impossible to guess what Irish would do in order to find his friend. Someone needed to keep an eye on him.

"Lance?"

"On it," Lance muttered in resignation, not happy to be given the babysitter task. "Does this mean I'm deputized?"

Mitch waited for Lance to be out of earshot before addressing Noah.

"I need your help."

"You got it."

Noah hadn't hesitated, but that would have been the same with any of Mitch's siblings.

"I want you to check Allie out of the B&B once Thorne gives the all clear for the guests to return to their rooms. She's with Dad at the moment, shopping for Halloween candy." Mitch figured he'd be given a shit ton of grief from Allie, but he'd rather deal with her wrath than be standing over her corpse. He planned to see her off first thing tomorrow morning. "You can take her stuff over to my place."

Allie had opted to take a shower at Mitch's place this morning, saying she'd use his washer and dryer for her clothes in order to make it through the day. Well, she'd be pleasantly surprised to find out that her belongings had personally been delivered—not. She'd wring his neck and then some.

"Is there any way that I can trade places with Lance?" Noah asked in jest, reaching for his phone to no doubt give Miles Schaeffer a call that he'd be delayed a bit this morning. They were both scheduled to be working up at the lake on the cottages, but that could wait a little longer. "You know, I don't need your favorite FBI agent to be mad at me, too…and I'm not talking about Thorne. I'm just saying it's not a good first impression for her to find out I'm the one who rifled through her personal belongings. Is there any chance she didn't unpack her suitcase yesterday? Would that be asking too much?"

In Mitch's opinion, at least that first impression would be possible.

Why had Allie made such a dangerous choice in flaunting her suitability as a target?

Sitting at his table in the kitchen across from her fresh from sleeping in his bed had clarified a few things for him—yes, he'd wanted her to come to town to help him solve these murders if she could, but he'd never gotten her completely out of his system.

Twelve months had passed since their night together, though they'd exchanged texts often enough. Neither one of them had brought up what happened after the fact, and it was like it had never transpired.

But it had.

And she would never settle for what he had to offer.

And if he was honest with himself, it wasn't enough. It had never been enough, and maybe he'd taken advantage of this chance to see if he'd made a mistake by walking away. Now all the consequences of his impetuous actions were coming home to roost. His inability to simply provide her security was resulting in a building anger, because she'd gone and blown any chance of that to hell with her decision to make herself a target.

"Don't worry about Allie." Mitch didn't want to get into the details of his decision or else Noah would make a bigger deal of the situation than was warranted. "I'll explain everything to her when I have time. She's off with Dad somewhere right now, and that's how I want to keep it until I can address this personally."

Noah feigned taking a step backward, causing Mitch to realize he'd given away more than he'd intended.

"Sheriff," Byron called out, saving Mitch from having to give Noah a lecture on adulthood. The deputy was weaving his way in and out of the crowd. "Sheriff, the background check you requested on Charlene Winston came over the wire."

Byron had a folder in his hand, but they were too close to the gathered horde of locals standing across the street. Mitch took the folder and began making his way back to the front yard of the inn. Thorne most likely had already received a SITREP regarding the latest victim in this case, but Mitch wasn't waiting on the feds to share their information.

"Byron, I'm going to need you to—"

Mitch had been going to give instructions to his deputy about tonight's Halloween festivities when he'd opened the manila folder.

Something wasn't right.

"Are you sure this report is accurate? What is our source?"

Mitch thumbed through the next two pages, taking in the highlighted notes that Byron had been keen enough to mark as vital to this investigation.

"It's mostly details from her employer and a quick internet search. It's what they had, which is why I figured you'd want to compare notes with Agent Thorne ASAP," Byron said as he looped his fingers into his belt. Mitch reflected on what was written down in front of him. Allie wasn't the first one to test their theory of how the suspect selected his victims during his hunt. "Charlene Winston didn't come from a broken home. She made it all up in hopes the killer would reach out to her."

"It seems her strategy worked," Mitch muttered, wondering what the reporter thought of her plan now. "Unfortunately, Charlene Winston might not live to write her own story."

CHAPTER TEN

"IT'S BEEN A while, Jay." Allie greeted her colleague with a guarded smile. Technically, Special Agent Jay Thorne worked out of the Cleveland office. The two of them rarely crossed paths anymore. They had both gone through the academy together, and she'd lucked out by getting assigned to Quantico in deference to her previous experience in military intelligence. It had been her dream delivered on a silver platter. "How've you been?"

Jay was sitting at one of the folding tables that was part of a longer chain of temporary desks. She was glad she'd picked a time when the other two agents assigned to the investigation were out and about scouring the town and running potential leads to ground on Charlene Winston's whereabouts.

"I'd be a lot better if you weren't standing in front of me right now, Delaney." Jay had always spoken his mind, and now was no exception. He was direct and to the point. It was part of what made him damned good at his job. He leaned back against the chair, allowing the wheels to roll him back from the table by a few inches. "I told Kendall to make sure you stayed far away from my investigation. Apparently, he didn't listen very well."

"Mitch called in a favor, and I couldn't say no." It was the truth, but Allie understood the ramifications of her involvement. It was the reason she was here. "I wanted to run something by you. If you're not interested, I'll fly back to D.C. No harm, no foul."

Jay remained silent as he hedged his bet. He no doubt recognized that she had nothing to lose in this situation and could walk away clean. She could have easily remained on the sidelines, given her two cents to a friend, and then headed back to her busy life on the East Coast.

She was standing in front of Jay because she could help advance the investigation.

"I know Kendall has been feeding you case files. If you have something that can help me, spit it out. Otherwise, Stringer is currently working on adding these latest developments to his ever-evolving profile." Jay pressed his thumb and index finger against his eyelids in exhaustion. This case had been overwhelming, but it was just one of many he would have to endure during his tenure. This eventuality was par for the course, because humanity didn't change. "You and I both know that Charlene Winston is most likely already dead."

"You're right, but it's not like you to throw in the towel." Allie pulled out one of the numerous chairs around the makeshift workspace. Files were stacked everywhere, a whiteboard was positioned in front of the table with a rather extensive timeline beset with hundreds of details and file numbers, and empty Styrofoam cups filled the trashcan. "I know you have something up your sleeve."

"Tell me what it is you've come to say, and then go spend time with your Marine buddy." Jay leaned forward and grabbed one of those empty Styrofoam cups—this one on the desk—to drain its cold contents before deciding on another. He pushed back his chair as he stood before walking the short distance to the coffee pot positioned on a side table. It was one of those old-fashioned units with two burners, but she doubted the orange glass carafe held the decaf coffee it was set aside for.

"I'm not in the mood for any games right now."

Neither was she.

Allie had spent the majority of the day with Gus, and had found herself enjoying every second of her time with Mitch's father. He was charming, intelligent, and backcountry wise when it came to life in general. To hear him tell it, people got in their own way too much and made everything way too complicated. She also didn't believe for half a second that he wasn't calling Mitch right this minute to rat her out.

The only saving grace she'd been afforded after walking through the station's doors was that the dispatcher hadn't been sitting at her desk. Allie wasn't certain that the woman would have allowed her past the main area of the police station without showing her credentials. She had no idea the disposition of the employee who guarded the gate, and she honestly didn't want to know.

There was a deputy whom Allie didn't recognize, but Mitch had mentioned he'd hired two new employees when he'd taken over as sheriff a couple of months ago. Or the man could have been Deputy Foster. She'd seen that name on the roster in one of the many reports she'd looked over since Mitch sent her the original case file.

The crew who had worked here under the old sheriff hadn't liked the way the old scheme was deposed, correctly calculating their chances of running their old scams on the new sheriff as next to none. A quick glance at the nameplate told her that the deputy was one of Mitch's new hires. He'd keep to himself.

Besides, she really wasn't worried about the deputy overhearing anything, seeing as he was across the room on the phone giving detailed directions to one of the town's older residents on how to unblock a garbage disposal.

"I figured out a way for you to trap the unsub in action."

Allie let her statement settle over Jay, whose hand hovered over his freshly brewed coffee. "Hear me out, Jay. Let's not waste time with politics."

Allie had already accepted that Mitch most likely would have sent her packing before first light tomorrow. It had never been his plan to draw her into the investigation, as much as he'd only intended to utilize her skillset. But he didn't get one without the other in her book. It wasn't how she normally operated, and Jay was a smart enough man to use the tools he had in front of him.

"You have one minute."

Jay picked up his coffee and walked back to his chair.

They both made themselves comfortable, but Allie wasn't sure she had that much time before Gus' message got through to Mitch about her current whereabouts. She had best get this party started.

"You're right that Mitch shouldn't have gone around you and called me in outside of the chain of command, but we've known each other for over sixteen years. He's actually a close friend. We spent time together under fire in Iraq and Afghanistan. I couldn't say no, and I had every intention of keeping my distance and only providing Mitch my insight over a couple of beers."

Allie leaned forward and rested her elbows on the table. She wasn't one of those people who bared her soul on social media, and she'd always been selective about who she allowed into her personal space. Mitch was one of the few, and only because of circumstances neither one of them had been able to avoid when serving together.

"I take it something changed in the last twenty-four hours?" Jay glanced down at the file he'd been studying when she'd walked into the station. "Did you know that the unsub was going to go after Charlene Winston?"

"I wasn't one hundred percent positive, but Shelby Til-madge's impromptu confession fast-forwarded the unsub's timeline." Allie figured Jay had already figured that one out, but no one could have foreseen the attack on a key player in the media, thereby sacrificing his access to the public. Maybe an angry letter or even an attempt to reach out by phone, but not an abduction. "You need to issue a press release. You need to drop the fact that Charlene Winston didn't come from a broken home, and you need to do it in a manner that isn't too conspicuous."

"I can't take that chance, and you know it. The unsub will kill her, if he hasn't already. He'll feel deceived and manipulated. He'll lash out at her and dump the mutilated body in the middle of Main Street as an example of what happens when law enforcement officials attempt to intervene in his life."

"No, he won't." Allie wasn't one hundred percent positive of that fact, but Charlene Winston was definitely going to die at some point if they didn't try something. "This unsub has only ever once veered off from his supposed sainthood project of building a family—Deputy Wallace."

"And he's six feet under, Allie, which tells me that the unsub doesn't care who he has to kill." Jay didn't bother to take a drink of coffee. He left the steaming cup on the table as he leaned back in his chair. "Your minute is up, although I do have a question. If you had been at the B&B last night, who do you think I'd be looking for today?"

"Fine. So, this isn't rocket science." Allie wasn't going to get Jay to see things her way unless she came totally clean, which she'd already decided to do before stepping foot inside the police station. She just had not expected that baring her soul to a colleague would be this hard. "I'm the unsub's ideal victim."

Jay blinked twice before slightly tilting his head to the side, almost as if he couldn't quite believe she'd capitulated so easily.

"I was raised by an alcoholic father. I ran away twice before I turned sixteen, and I had my dad sign off on a parental consent form so I could enlist. He signed so that I could go into the Marines at the age of seventeen." Allie summed her life up as if she were the subject of a random profile note. She didn't often dwell on her past, because it had no bearing on her future. She'd accepted that long ago. "Jay, we know that the unsub prefers younger victims who were abandoned early in their lives or led a troubled life. That changed when he chose to abduct Whitney Bell. She was older, but her alcoholic father failed her. It was his failing health that brought her back to town. Age no longer matters. The unsub is hurt that the residents can't recognize his genuine need for a family, he's angry that everything he's built has been dismantled, and worst of all…he's lonely. His family has been taken from him."

The lines of various telephones around the station continued to ring before either rolling over to what Allie assumed was the county's 911 system or to voicemail. The hum of the mini-refrigerator drowned out the steady hiss of the coffee machine, but all the droning resonances of the station couldn't hide Jay's sigh of acknowledgment.

"And what? You're the perfect sister he never had?"

Allie allowed Jay to have his moment of witticism, but the fact that he didn't kick her out of the police station told her that he recognized the benefit of what she was offering.

"I've inadvertently laid the groundwork." Okay, so Allie had definitely stretched the truth there, but the foundation had been laid all the same. "We're all on the same page when it comes to the outline of the unsub's identity. He's embedded in this town. As of today, there isn't a resident in Blyth Lake who doesn't know that I come from a single parent home and that I used the military as a way to get out."

Jay ran a hand over his face as he considered the ramifications of screwing this up, and it didn't surprise her when he stood and began to pace while clicking the end of the pen in his hand. He'd done the same thing back when they were in the academy and working on one the various scenarios given to them by their instructors.

"It's not the usual way we do things, Allie." Jay was most likely considering the fallout of such a plan. It was a solid lead, and he would eventually come to the right conclusion. "I have to ask—whose idea was this?"

"It sure as hell wasn't mine," Mitch exclaimed in anger as he barged into the station. She'd heard the small buzzer that indicated someone had walked through the door, and she didn't need to turn around to know who it was. This confrontation was bound to happen, but she'd done what she'd set out to do—give Special Agent Jay Thorne the option of using her in an official capacity. "Thorne, disregard everything you've just heard. Allie is leaving first thing in the morning, and we're going to remain behind and work this case the way we've been—"

"And where exactly is that getting you?" Allie interjected, standing to her feet and facing the man who'd brought her to this tiny little town. "Why are we going back and forth on this, Ken? You called me for one reason only—to help you catch this son of a bitch who'd been terrorizing young girls for over a decade. I'm here. I'm standing right in front of you and offering—"

"You're offering yourself up as some sort of sacrificial lamb, and you damn well know the killer has the initiative."

Mitch was completely focused on her, ignoring the fact there were other people in the station. The deputy had clearly finished up his phone call and didn't feign disinterest on what was happening across the room. She wasn't going to have this confrontation spiral out of control when the answer was right in front of their faces.

"I'm doing the job you asked me to do, Mitch," Allie replied quietly, refusing to be drawn into an argument where there didn't have to be one.

She'd purposefully used his nickname, which she rarely exercised when addressing him. Hell, the last time she'd said his given name had been when they were in her bed that night. The way his blue eyes had become heated lasers told she'd done her job in halting an argument that had a real chance of getting completely out of control.

"In case either of you have forgotten, Allie was never assigned to this case." Jay pulled both of their attentions his way as he stood in front of the whiteboard with too many young faces on display. "With that said, she's got an idea that could possibly save some lives."

It was impossible to miss the way Mitch's jawline became taut in his attempt to restrain his reply. Maybe she hadn't done such a good job in diffusing his anger.

Without thinking, Allie stepped forward and took ahold of Mitch's hand. She waited until he dragged his heated gaze from Jay to focus on her.

"You're allowing this to become personal," Allie said softly, needing him to take a step back from their friendship. "It's pretty simple. You called me, I'm here, and Jay can spin my involvement with his supervisor so that we can wrap up this darkness that has fallen over your town. I'm not understanding why you can't recognize that, Mitch."

He studied her carefully as he tightened his grip on her hand. He'd always been stubborn, but that gesture alone should have told her that it would take more than a few sentences to convince him to see things her way. She never expected what came next.

"You're the one not truly understanding things here, Allie." Mitch pulled her even closer as he leaned down so that only she could hear his words. He was attempting to once again change the foundation of their friendship, and she wasn't so sure she didn't want to follow his lead. "This *is* personal for me."

CHAPTER ELEVEN

"**I**F YOU GRIT your teeth any harder, you'll be swallowing a mouthful of broken enamel."

Gwen wasn't able to cover up her wince of discomfort with a smile fast enough as she took a seat on the porch. Even the dim yellow bug light his father had put in the fixture next to the front door couldn't hide the fact that the stitches in her side still bothered her.

In the span of twenty-four hours, old feelings had resurfaced that he'd long since thought had been put to rest. He and Allie both agreed that they made better friends than lovers. It had been a mutual agreement given the circumstances at the time. He still believed that they'd made the right choice, but his heart had other ideas. She wasn't just city through and through. She was big city to the limit. There was no changing that.

Hell, Allie's entire personal and professional life revolved in or immediately around D.C.

She might commute daily to Quantico, but she craved the busy streets, the culture, the nightlife, and her exclusive circle of tight lifelong friends. It was all she'd known growing up, and it was doubtful that she'd ever want to leave.

"You know, we can drive Allie to your house after dessert if you need to head back into town to issue marching orders for the evening shift tonight," Gwen offered, curling her legs underneath herself as she settled into the cushion. "I can only imagine that Agent Thorne and his team are working around the clock to figure out where Charlene Winston has been taken. With every child in town out hunting for the best treats on Halloween, you might just have your hands full."

"No, I'll take Allie home."

Mitch hadn't told his family yet of the plan that Allie, Jay, and the agent's team had worked on while the earlier round of trick or treaters marched through town collecting pieces of candy from the various shops on Main Street prior to the big event tonight. Even though nearly every shop had participated and the event had gone off without a hitch, there hadn't been a parent who'd been smiling throughout the evening.

Everyone was on high alert.

All thoughts were on the fact that another woman had gone missing right under their noses, and neither the sheriff's department nor the FBI had any idea of how to find her.

"I know it's none of my business, but you were the one who in fact invited Allie here to Blyth Lake. I know she's an old friend you thought could help you catch this son of a bitch, but the least you could do is be nice to her while she's still here." Gwen pulled her jacket tighter around her neck when a gust of wind blew some leaves across the old wooden porch. "You've had a frown on your face since you walked through the door…without the required side dish, I might add."

Mitch refrained from snapping at his sister that he hadn't had time to bake a side dish with the recent abduction and all, but she didn't deserve his wrath. She'd been through enough personally, and he needed to focus on the problems at hand. Besides, she'd only made mention of it in jest to get him to lighten his mood. Unfortunately, that wasn't going to happen until he could put Allie in a car or a plane where she'd be safe and sound.

"Allie has Dad wrapped around her pinky finger," Mitch said, staring out into the dark abyss. Not even a sliver of a crescent moon had dared grace the darkness of this Halloween. "He doesn't even realize I stepped outside."

"Allie will when she smells that damn cigarette smoke on you." Gwen raised an eyebrow as if she'd succeeded in catching Mitch red-handed revisiting a habit he'd kicked long ago. He refrained from calling it a filthy practice, because cigarettes had gotten him through some tough times in Corps. "By the way, I like her."

"I'm glad to hear it, but as for lighting up a cig…I haven't smoked since the day I signed my papers."

"I'm just teasing you, dear brother." Gwen sighed and turned her head toward the screen door. "I wish I'd thought to bring us out some coffee, though. I didn't want to interrupt Dad. He was busy telling Allie stories of when you wanted to grow up to be G.I. Joe."

"At the rate he tells that shaggy dog, we won't be having coffee until tomorrow morning." Mitch would have gone inside to get his sister that cup of coffee she wanted, but it was just his luck that he received a text message. One glance told him all he needed to know. "Let's head inside. There's something—"

"Mitch!"

"Hey, you two," Noah said, sticking his head out the screened door. Did he really think that they hadn't heard Lance's bellow? "Breaking news on the television."

Mitch took the few steps to the loveseat that his parents always sat on together when enjoying the cooler weather in the evenings. Gwen smiled her appreciation as she took ahold of his hand, using him as leverage to stand.

"You don't look surprised," Gwen noted, taking a step ahead of him and brushing past Noah. "Whatever is going on,

Mitch, you can tell us. We have your back."

Mitch caught Allie's gaze, and he could see that she figured out what was about to be announced on the local television station. Had Lance used the remote to switch to a national one, the result would have been the same—a press release giving an update on Charlene Winston, which was purposefully worded to include that both of her parents were worried sick over her abduction.

"I know you do, sis." Mitch wasn't surprised to see Chad cross the room to come stand behind Gwen. "But I'm sheriff, and this isn't on you. Enjoy your homecoming, let your man take care of you, and work up a retirement plan for me...I don't want to be dealing with this shit in my sixties."

Mitch had always told his siblings that there wasn't anything so horrible in life that it couldn't be fixed with a simple choice.

He'd been wrong.

A simple phone call to an old friend had spiraled out of control, and there didn't seem to be a damned thing he could do to change the upcoming course of events. This press release was only the beginning of their gambit.

"Shit," Lance muttered, watching the news as he whipped out his cell phone. No doubt that he was texting Brynn, who was at The Cavern tonight and couldn't make dinner. From what Mitch heard, she and Allie had already met. Or Lance could have been reaching out to Irish. "This isn't a good development."

"Mitch, is there something you want to fill us all in on?" Jace asked from his spot next to Shae. The two of them were on one side of the couch, while Reese Woodward sat on the other end where Noah was resting a hand on her shoulder. "It's not like we're not all in on this together."

Mitch met Allie's gaze, and he wasn't surprised when she shook her head in the minimalist manner. No one else caught her slight warning, but he understood the dangerous terrain they'd begun to travel on as per this afternoon's plan.

His family had been thrown a lot with each homecoming, and he had a decision to make.

Allie wasn't going to like the choice he made and neither was Thorne. They weren't used to the inner workings of a small town, but Mitch had figured out a way to keep his family at bay while allowing this new plan he didn't actually agree with unfold.

"There's been a shift in the investigation, and Allie will be an integral part of the case on her visit here in Blyth Lake." Everyone began to speak at once, so Mitch held up his hand so that he could finish his announcement. He wanted this over and done with so that he could take Allie back to his house and finally have a conversation that they'd both ignored for too long. "I trust Agent Thorne as the lead investigator on this manhunt, and so should you. As far as you are all concerned, nothing has changed and nothing is to be said outside of this house. Agreed?"

By this time, Allie had crossed her arms and was studying everyone's reaction. Her attention seemed to linger on Lance the longest, which wasn't a surprise. He would be the most vocal when it came to being kept in the dark.

Mitch's speech would no doubt be taken out of context by nearly everyone present. He had made it sound as if Allie would be officially helping in her role as a profile when in actuality she was basically being used as bait to catch a killer. Eventually, one of his siblings would figure it out…most likely Gwen would be the most circumspect. She tended to be observant of potential speech indicators and body language more quickly than the others.

"Could we have a word in private?" Gus asked quietly as he nodded toward the kitchen. "There's something you should know. Noah, could you watch the door for more trick or treaters, please?"

Mitch's day hadn't gone quite as planned, and he wasn't looking forward to more bad news. Whatever his father had to say most likely had to do with the case. Unfortunately, there were certain questions that Mitch wasn't at liberty to answer.

"Of course." Mitch ignored the twinge that had settled in his hip around sixteen hundred hours. That was the usual time when he began to feel the dull ache inhabit the muscles surrounding the pins, plates, and screws his service had left him with. Standing all day certainly didn't help him in that regard. "Let me just tell Allie that we're heading out in five minutes."

Mitch crossed the room to do just that, but she was already engaged in conversation with Chad now that the broadcast was over. The discussion was regarding the bonfire he'd thrown the fateful night that Emma Irwin had gone missing. The man had probably told that story a thousand times since then, so it had probably become rather rote in the consistency. Hell, Mitch could recite the tale by this point. He considered it a dry well by now.

"Five minutes," Mitch murmured to Allie, nodding an apology to Chad for the interruption. "Dad just wants to have a quick word with me."

"Is everything alright?" Allie must have witnessed the concern Gus had displayed, but there wasn't anything Mitch could say to alleviate her concern until he spoke with his dad. It was probably nothing and just a word of caution that a father would relay to a son, anyway. "I can—"

"I've got it covered. Let Chad finish his story." Mitch gave her a small smile even though he was still struggling to accept that she'd gone to Thorne instead of talking to him first. "I'll be right back."

It didn't take long for Mitch to reach the kitchen, and memories of his mother surrounded him in a familiar, warm embrace.
Lace doily white curtains were still hanging from the rod above
the sink, a stack of her crocheted pot holders were still next to
the stove on the counter, and a small barrel cactus that Lance
had gotten at school and given to her sometime back in
elementary school was still alive and flourishing in the window-
sill. Who would've guessed her plant would still be around all
these years later?

Mitch figured everything would remain in the same place
until the day their father died, which by the grace of God
wouldn't be for a very long time to come.

"What's on your mind, Dad?"

"I wanted to make sure Gwen talked to you while the two of
you were out on the porch." Gus reached over one of the
kitchen chairs to where the same old toothpick holder his father
had used for as long as Mitch could remember rested on top a
lazy Susan his mother had picked up at a flea market. "I'm
worried about her."

Mitch had already known his day wasn't going to get any
better, but he sure as hell was hoping it couldn't get worse.

"Gwen didn't mention anything of significance to me when
we talked," Mitch reluctantly admitted, casting a look in the
direction of the living room. "What's going on?"

Gus' audible sigh of frustration was telling, and Mitch steeled
himself for another blow.

"Gwen has been having nightmares regarding her attack."
Gus held up a hand. "Now before you say that it's a normal
occurrence for someone after suffering an attack like that, you
should also know that she recognizes the face of the killer in her
dreams."

CHAPTER TWELVE

"I NEVER DID like the silent treatment," Allie said as she walked through the front door of Mitch's home, unable to stand the enforced silence anymore. The car ride would have been made in relative peace had he not come across as a powder keg ready to explode. "It's like shunning me after I got thrown off the island. You know better than anyone that this is a way to bring an end to the investigation. We all make sacrifices in order to accomplish the mission. Does that sound familiar?"

The blazer she'd been wearing had been perfect to keep the cold at bay during the day, but it hadn't been heavy enough for the cold front that seemed to have settled over the area after the trick or treaters had gone in for the night. She didn't bother to take it off as she turned around to get this brewing confrontation out of the way. The sooner the better, as far as she was concerned.

"What I know is that you purposefully put yourself in harm's way on a case that isn't even yours in the first place." Mitch punched the alarm code into the small square panel before he closed the front door. He then flipped the deadbolt into place with a flick of his wrist. "I didn't ask you to come to town so that you could risk your life. I requested your expertise in profiling onsite. The delays were costing us valuable time. Last time I checked, profiling didn't require field work. To top it off, my sister is having nightmares about her own boyfriend turning out to be the unsub."

Mitch walked past her and into the kitchen without another word.

Oh yeah. He was angry.

"Gwen replacing the man in her dreams with Chad tells me that her mind is attempting to reconstruct details about the night she was attacked. The unsub is familiar to all of you, and her mind is trying to piece everything together in a way that makes some kind of sense. It certainly doesn't mean Chad did anything wrong."

Mitch didn't bother to reply to her rationalization, leaving her no choice but to follow him into the kitchen if she wanted to continue this conversation. They needed to get things out in the open or else his anger would continue to fester. Dragging this thing out wasn't in anyone's best interest.

"Thorne called his supervisor, I contacted mine, and everyone is in agreement that this plan can work. It's the best option available to us as it stands right now, Mitch. Even you can see that it's obvious." Allie stopped and leaned against the side of the archway between the living room and the kitchen as Mitch began to set the coffee maker for the morning. At first, she thought he was actually making a fresh pot at twenty-two hundred hours. It wasn't until he began to adjust the timer that she realized he was programming the appliance for tomorrow morning. Some habits were just ingrained into their human nature, and the same went for the unsub they were tracking, regardless of how far out of civilized behavior he'd pushed himself. "The facts stand for themselves. The unsub has most likely been told time and time again that I'm a friend of yours visiting from D.C. It only stands to reason that you move me out of the inn to stay here. You would do that for—"

"For who, Allie?" Mitch wasn't taking any prisoners tonight, but she didn't need him to coddle her. Everything was already written up, turned in, and ready to execute. Besides, this was what she was trained to do. "I would do that for who? A woman I'm involved with? A woman I care about? Who would I go to such lengths for in order to keep someone away from this sadistic fuck's grasp, huh?"

"We both know that you would go the extra mile for a virtual stranger," Allie reluctantly admitted, but she wasn't about to let him steer her off course with such provocative questions. They needed to cover their own groundwork to ensure the plan they'd put together with Thorne wasn't all for naught. Mitch had been there against his objections, insisting on certain safeguards and refusing to give her too much rope. He was part of the plan whether he liked it or not. "Let's not beat around the bush. We're talking about the fact that the town believes we're involved. Regardless that you told them I'm here as a friend who might be able to give you some insight into the investigation, it doesn't matter either way. These residents believe we're involved, and they'll have even more faith in that assumption when you spend every waking moment with me that you're not spending at the station—as we've done already to this point. The unsub will begin to believe that I could be a viable target, just as he believed with Gwen. He'll eventually make his move. He wants a victim who fits his narrative."

Allie wondered how blue eyes could become so dark, but she'd witnessed the change herself many times before. Her heart fluttered at the manner of intensity in which he carefully observed her reaction to his inquiry.

"And did it ever occur to you that we might not come back from this? That it might do permanent damage to our relationship?"

Twelve months.

That's how much time had passed since they'd slept together. Numerous texts and emails had been sent to maintain their friendship, but never once had either one of them brought up the night that could have potentially ruined what they had between them.

He was wading into unchartered waters that they'd both agreed to steer clear of. As long as they continued the course they'd previously chosen, they would be fine.

Right?

"This isn't…"

Allie wasn't so sure what she'd been going to say, so she let her voice trail off as she took time to gather her thoughts.

"This isn't like last time?" Mitch had his arms crossed over his chest, and she'd stopped breathing for just a second when he lowered them to his sides. She exhaled slowly, albeit unsteadily, when he remained where he was. It was better they keep a bit of space between them when they were alone like this. The attraction between them hadn't simmered in the least, and somehow the pull had only become stronger. "I can still feel your warm lips on mine, Allie."

Her body flushed with arousal with his vivid admission.

He'd steered the fucking boat right over the falls, and she was barely hanging on to the marker buoy.

"Mitch, we agreed—"

"Every time I heard your voice on the phone, it was all I could do not to book myself a flight back to Washington." Mitch took that first step toward her hanging there on the precipice, but she held her ground in impressive fashion. They'd gone over these same falls before and come out the other end in one piece. They could do so again. "In the past twenty-four hours, every time you've called me by my nickname…I wanted to remind you of the time you called out my given name. That should mean something to you, too."

Allie could barely swallow around the constriction in her throat, but she managed as she straightened her shoulders. He'd been the only man to truly breach her defenses, and she'd chalked it up to the years they'd known each other. There was a very fine line between friendship and intimacy between a man and a woman.

They'd crossed it once and managed to survive the fallout.

She changed her mind about a second trip, though.

She wasn't sure they'd be able to do it twice and survive.

"Do you remember what you said to me the following morning?" Allie needed him to remember their brief exchange, because nothing had changed since that time. Right? She hated that she was second guessing herself, but now she wasn't so sure after he'd taken another step closer. She quickly spoke to stop him in his tracks. "Let me refresh your memory. You said that we were far too different to be anything other than friends. And we are, Mitch. We're on completely opposite ends of the spectrum."

Mitch was now only inches from where she stood in the archway of his kitchen. She wasn't about to take a step back, so she tilted her head to meet his blue-eyed gaze. What in the world had ever caused her to think that one night with him would be enough?

Time and distance had been the answer, and those were both gone.

That didn't stop her from trying to protect both of them one last time.

"We both know that I'm not cut out for a serious commitment," Allie managed to whisper, still holding firm to her precious self-identity. "I saw firsthand tonight the reason you came home to Blyth Lake. Your father, brothers, and sister are who center you. They keep you grounded. I don't know the first thing about long term relationships or being the woman you'd want me to be. My longest affair lasted just three and a half months, and that was only because I was working a case and didn't have time to call things off when we were done. The closest thing I have to family is a pigeon who visits my balcony every evening around dinnertime to catch a few croutons from my salad."

Allie gave Mitch credit.

He'd listened to every word she said before reaching out to touch her.

"Don't," Allie warned, turning her face slightly so that he couldn't touch her cheek. She could get through this with what remained of her integrity and their friendship intact, despite the fact that she wanted nothing more than to feel his calloused hands on her body once again. "Nothing material has changed. Nothing."

Allie didn't wait for Mitch to agree. There wasn't anything else she could say to make him see reason tonight, and she didn't view the fact that she left him standing there in the archway between the kitchen and the living room as retreating. She was giving them both space to accept the line they'd both drawn in the sand so many months ago.

With each stride she took toward the staircase came a lingering fear that he would stop her, but also a deep-seated dread that he wouldn't reach out.

This was what she'd wanted, right? She'd told herself many times over the course of this past year that the deepest core of who she was had been engrained in her long ago. It had been her anchor, unmoving and forever present.

She didn't know the first thing about commitment, other than to her job.

So why, then, did a burning hot exhilaration wash over her when he wrapped his large, calloused hand around her wrist? His grasp was one that caused her to pause, but not tight enough that she couldn't continue if she'd wanted to. Her palms were flush with the soft fabric of his shirt lying against his chest in an instant, and even the thick material couldn't hide his broad muscles underneath.

Every nerve awakened throughout her body when Mitch didn't even bother to use words in an attempt to convince her that she was wrong to cling to that anchor.

Instead, he kissed her.

He kissed her in such a fiery, passionate and familiar manner that it was as if their one weekend together had never ended. Their tongues became reunited in an exotic dance as their breaths became one. She didn't want to admit it, but it was as if she'd been lost…and she'd once again found her home.

"Say my name," Mitch murmured as he picked her up, not giving her a choice but to wrap her legs around his waist.

"Mitch," Allie whispered, giving him what he wanted. There was absolutely no way she could deny him or her own desires. Who was she kidding? She'd join him in his bed every night until this investigation came to a close, but they both knew the unspoken truth—she'd eventually go back to her life in D.C. "Take me to bed, Mitch."

"About fucking time," Mitch muttered, crushing his lips to hers as he expertly managed the stairs without so much as a misstep. "Don't think the discussion regarding your involvement in this case has been tabled. It hasn't."

Allie didn't think for a second that Mitch was done giving a lecture about the dangers of her job, the threat to her safety, and the status of their relationship. It was in his nature to have the last word, but his bark was a hell of lot worse than his bite…well, in most instances.

When his teeth lightly bit the cord of her neck, she'd definitely experienced the arousal shoot straight to her core. She laid her head back to give him better access and was rewarded with the heat of his tongue.

It didn't take them long to reach his bedroom, and he didn't waste time closing the bedroom door. He did manage to flip the switch as they crossed the threshold, but it didn't turn on the overhead light. Instead, it was one of those switches that controlled a bedside lamp.

The golden hue didn't even have a chance to cast its light over the room before her feet touched the ground. His fingers were already on the button of her blazer, and she gently placed her hand over his.

They both understood how this visit was going to end.

Allie just wanted to relish every second they had while she was still in town.

"Let me," Allie said quietly, taking over his task and slowly slipping the button through the opening. She never took her gaze off his as she let the heavy fabric fall down her shoulders. The blue of his eyes was practically the same color as the heart of a fire, and she could literally sense the heat on her skin. "Will you…"

Allie didn't need to finish her question. Mitch was already holding out an open palm for her firearm. It didn't take long for her to unclip the holster and gently set them in his hand. He walked around the side of the bed and set both of their weapons side by side on the only nightstand.

Mitch then held out his hand. The sweet gesture had her heart fluttering all over again and prompted her to take the last few steps to where he was standing. He then quietly sat on the bed, his solid weight dipping the mattress. She remained standing in front of him as she gradually took the bottom of her turtleneck and lifted the soft material over her head.

Her hairband slipped out and joined her shirt on the floor.

She didn't stop there, though. Wanton desire glistened in his heated gaze, and the temperature in the room rose by several degrees.

God, she'd missed being with him.

"Don't stop on my account," Mitch murmured, already half done with unbuttoning his dress shirt. "Have I mentioned that you have the most sensual body I've ever had the pleasure of touching...or seeing...or..."

"I get the drift," Allie said with a light laugh as he reached out and tugged her hand with enough force that he had to cradle her fall to the bed. Somehow, he managed to turn them so that she was lying on her back. "I wasn't done, Ken."

"Ken isn't here right now," Mitch warned her with an arched eyebrow. He then leaned down to press his lips against the cleavage spilling out from her bra. She was hoping he'd do more than that, but he pulled away despite her disagreeing moan. "Let's get these boots off of you."

Mitch was good on his promise, and that wasn't an easy feat considering the boots she wore were knee-high. They were both still laughing when the second heel landed to the floor with a clunk.

"Now, where were we?" Mitch asked as he took a step back and continued to unfasten the buttons on his shirt. Allie couldn't tear her gaze away from the tantalizing view before her as he finally revealed his muscular shoulders, then his biceps, and then...his fingers pulled out the material of the tank style t-shirt he'd worn underneath his shirt from the waistband of his jeans. "Allie?"

"I'm just enjoying the show," Allie admitted quietly, not

wanting to ruin the moment. It was apparent he'd kept up his daily workout routine. Otherwise, he wouldn't have had those washboard abs she loved so much. She lifted a corner of her lip to let him know he still had her attention. "It's good to see that you're still keeping fit."

Mitch had never been one to take a compliment, and he didn't do so now. His sole focus was on her, so she didn't disappoint him. She slipped her thumbs inside the unzipped waistband of her jeans and slowly pulled the denim down over her hips, exposing her matching set of panties.

Her bra and underwear weren't made of lace or been worn to draw the attention of the opposite sex, but it didn't seem to matter much to the man before her. Mitch didn't even bother to take his jeans off as he waited until hers hit the floor. She hadn't even drawn breath before his hands were resting on the bed, positioned on both sides of her head.

"You're the most beautiful woman, inside and out." Mitch lightly pressed his lips to hers, not bothering to close his eyes. There was something erotic about having him watching her reactions so closely. "I've missed you, Allie."

Without another word, Mitch began to love every square inch of her body. His lips caressed her neck and shoulders as he lowered the straps on her bra. She couldn't help but arch her back so that he could expertly unfasten the hooks with one hand. Talk about a practiced talent.

The cool air brushed over her nipples, but the intense sensation was nothing to when he drew one of her nubs into the heat of his mouth. It was when he brushed his tongue over the tip that she had to dig her heels into the edge of the mattress.

"Yes," Allie managed to hiss out between clenched teeth. She lifted her hands above her head in order to grab the comforter for something to hold on to. She knew from experience that he would take his time with her breasts before continuing downward to her core. "More…"

Mitch was now tracing his tongue down her abdomen to the edge of her black underwear, which somehow miraculously began to be pulled down her legs. She certainly wasn't going to stop the progression of pleasure. With each inch downward, his lips followed.

Allie couldn't stop the groan of ecstasy from leaving her lips when he remembered how sensitive her inner ankle was on her left foot. That was not the kind of thing that friends were supposed to know, but she shoved that small problem away from her thoughts for another time that would certainly come around sooner than either of them wanted.

"I'll give you as much pleasure as you'd like," Mitch said before settling in between her legs and doing just that. "My name falling from your lips is going to be my reward."

He tenderly kissed each of her inner thighs, slowly licked each fold, and even ever-so-gently used his middle finger to breach her opening. Never once did he touch her clit, which only made her bundle of nerves swell even more.

"Mitch…"

Apparently, her soft moan of his given name wasn't enough.

He continued to indulge himself without ever stroking her clit until he had somehow brought her right to the edge of that steep precipice. Every part of her body was primed for the fall, but she was left hovering over the abyss.

"Please," Allie begged, tightening her grip on the comforter as she strived for the pleasure only he could give her. "Mitch, please!"

Allie exploded the moment his warm lips covered her clit and the brush of his tongue created a burning path straight into euphoria. Her back arched to accept the waves of desire that continued to wash over her as lights danced behind the lashes she'd closed against the blissful fall.

His name being called out over and over again began to penetrate the rushing blood through her ears. She was the one chanting and hadn't realized that her response was the one he'd remembered from before. He was right. She'd intimately called him by his given name in throes of passion.

And this time...she couldn't blame the tequila.

CHAPTER THIRTEEN

"**W**E HAVE THIRTY more minutes before that alarm goes off," Mitch said without bothering to open his eyes. It was still dark outside anyway, and they'd shut the light off a couple of hours ago. "You can't tell me that you're not tired."

"How could you possibly know that we still have thirty minutes?"

Allie's warm body was pressed tightly against his, but her head was tilted too far back on his shoulder for her to be sleeping comfortably. The weight of her stare through the shadows for the last five minutes told him that this latest development between them was weighing heavily on her mind.

He wasn't ready to discuss this sharp turn in their relationship, either.

Hardly anything ever truly frightened him, with the exception of losing his family. But Allie? Her foregone conclusions about their future scared the shit out of him.

"It's five thirty-one."

Allie shifted so that she could look over him toward the neon red clock next to their firearms. He couldn't help but smile.

"How did you do that?"

"You should know by now how talented I am," Mitch said against her neck as he rolled her over onto her back. "Seriously, we're running on like two hours of sleep and today is going to be hell after that press release Thorne issued."

Allie tensed slightly at the mention of the workday, but she slowly relaxed as he began to kiss her temple and then work his way down behind her ear.

"I'm surprised we're not running out of condoms," Allie muttered, wrapping her legs around his waist. His throbbing shaft rested in between her folds, and he would have given anything to work himself inside of her without a barrier. That wasn't smart on either one of their parts, so he reached underneath the pillow where he'd stored the few remaining foiled discs. "You need to put those on your grocery list, although I'm certain that will make the news."

Mitch didn't ponder long over her request, but it did slip across his thoughts that it was one way to catch the attention of the residents in this town. Blyth Lake had a small pharmacy tucked in between the bakery and an antique store that he'd yet to step foot in since his return, but maybe that would change later today. Allie by his side while they purchased a crate or two of condoms would no doubt have the locals talking up a storm.

"Hey," Allie whispered, resting her hand on the side of his face. She couldn't hide her concern, either. "Let's just take this one minute at a time."

Mitch used his teeth to tear the foil and remove the condom. He pushed the outside world to the back burner so that he could focus on what was in front of him—Allie. He wasn't the type of man who took the day minute by minute, but he'd indulge both of them for the time being.

He rolled the latex over his cock and rested his tip against her entrance. She lifted both of her legs until they were wrapped around his waist, bringing his body closer to hers.

Would he ever get enough of her?

Mitch leaned down just enough so that his chest was pressed to hers, needing as much contact with her warmth as he could get…he wasn't sure how soon the empty cold would seep into his bed.

He didn't rush this moment. Instead, he ever so slowly worked his way inside of her until her heated sheath was wrapped snugly around his shaft. He closed his eyes and rested his cheek against hers, staying locked in place to savor this unending intimacy.

Their breathing eventually became uneven as the building arousal eventually stole their patience. He gradually pulled out until he could begin all over again. He settled into a rhythm, using deliberate thrusts that weren't too fast or too slow. Time passed slowly as he continued to love her, both of them eventually falling into each other's embrace as pleasure consumed them both.

"YOU'RE MITCH'S FRIEND, aren't you?"

Allie had been searching for an open booth at the diner when the question caught her off guard. She and Mitch had agreed to meet for lunch today when both of them had been using the shower at once to conserve water. At least, that's what they'd told themselves to justify their continued playfulness.

She didn't believe for a second that they weren't fooling each other about last night, but the consequences of their actions would come later—enough of a later that she didn't need to think about it right now. He'd texted her mid-morning to let her know that there were no new developments concerning Charlene Winston. The good part to that was no one had stumbled across her body. The bad part, obviously, was that Charlene was still missing and in the hands of a serial murderer.

Had the unsub killed Charlene and found himself a new gravesite? Or was he now torn after hearing that press release?

Did he realize he'd destroyed an undeserving woman?

They most likely wouldn't receive the answers they sought anytime soon.

Hence today's outing.

"Yes, I'm Allie Delaney."

The diner was full of life, with numerous patrons talking over one another and clanks of silverware being scraped across plates. The sound of meat sizzling on the grill could be heard from the open kitchen, and two waitresses were handling the busy lunch hour with grace—one of them being Molly Stewart.

"I'm Rose Phifer." She could easily pass for a woman in her early forties, though Allie knew her to be much older. At least, according to the case file. Rose and Tiny Phifer were the loving couple who'd taken Brynn in after she'd lost her parents. "This is my husband, Tiny. Please join us."

Allie came close to declining their offer, wanting to have Mitch to herself for a little longer. Unfortunately, the importance of the case overruled her needs.

"Thank you," Allie said, returning the woman's smile. Handshakes were exchanged and it wasn't long before she was settled in one of the two remaining chairs. "Mitch should be along to join us shortly. He got held up at the station, I'm guessing."

"Is there any word on that reporter?" Tiny asked in concern, his voice so deep it reminded her of that one entertainer who could memorize people by simply reading a grocery list. Allie thought Mitch was tall at around six feet, but this man was literally a giant like those guys in pro-wrestling. "I've been thinking that the killer revealed too much in one of those letters he's been sending her way. Maybe that's why he snatched her up. I'm sure Mitch and those federal agents already thought of that, though."

"Mitch texted me a little bit ago that they didn't have any

new developments," Allie shared, taking the napkin out from underneath the silverware. She draped the white paper over her lap, not needing to glance around the diner to know that several gazes had landed on her presence at the table. "It's horrible what's been happening here in this beautiful town. Watching all the youngsters march around in their costumes yesterday made me wonder what it would have been like to grow up here in Blyth Lake."

Rose reached for her coffee, causing her bracelets to give off a charming melody. She had a calming presence that immediately told Allie the woman was a peacemaker, an empathizer, and that she cared for those around her. Her gaze had softened the second Tiny had brought up Charlene's status.

"It *is* horrible. I'll tell you, we've lived here all our lives." Rose paused to take a sip of her hot tea, holding the string aside with her index finger. "Blyth Lake was the most peaceful town in existence until this monster came in and took from us everything we held dear."

Tiny shook his head as he stared into the depth of the coffee cup as if it held the key to turning back time.

Maybe he could.

Before Allie could jog Tiny's memory, Molly came out of nowhere with a tray of cold drinks.

"Afternoon, Allie." Molly set down a glass filled with ice and what looked like Coke. "I figured Mitch is joining you, so I already placed your orders. Tiny and Rose, your plates should be out in about three minutes."

"Now that's service," Allie complimented with a smile. She wanted to ask what had been ordered, but she'd never been put in this type of position before and decided she'd just fall in line with the local routine. Breakfast and lunch were two entirely different meals, so how had Molly known what Allie would have ordered? Occupations such as waitressing and bartending were very similar to profiling, because those types of personnel were observers. But they weren't mind readers, so how had Molly known that Allie had been going to order a soda? "Thank you, Molly. By the way, I met your son the other day over at Mitch's house."

"Really?" Molly seemed truly in the dark about Jack's short visit. She tilted her head as she waited for an answer. "What was Jack doing over there at Mitch's place?"

"Oh, it was nothing. Jack was just concerned about Shelby and thought that Mitch should know." Allie waited for Molly to move on to the next table before continuing on the same path of the conversation. "Shelby is around Jack's age, right? Did they go to school together? It was nice that Jack was looking out for his welfare."

Tiny's sideways glance and upturned lip told Allie more than if she'd directed her question toward the man himself. She slid the straw off the table and began to take the wrapper off.

"Jack was more than a handful when he was young," Tiny said, keeping a soft tone so that Molly couldn't overhear him. His attempt at privacy didn't get very far, especially seeing as the couple in the booth across from them was listening to every word. "That boy only ever thinks of himself. As for Shelby, let's just say that he was taught at home more than he ever attended public school."

"I never thought Shelby was the killer in the first place," the man in the booth said before taking another bite of his sandwich. He chewed, swallowed, and then wiped his mouth with a napkin. "If you ask me, I don't think it's anyone living here in this town. I think this monster has got all of you feds fooled. A neighbor wouldn't do so something so horrible to another neighbor."

"I agree," the woman exclaimed, leaning forward to get in her two cents worth. She must have had her hair done this morning, because there wasn't a strand out of place in the net of hairspray. Her greyish eyes were directed straight at Allie. "You're Mitch's friend, right? The woman from the FBI headquarters?"

"Yes, Mitch and I go way back." Allie pulled her glass closer and dipped the straw in between the ice cubes. "We were in the Marines together."

"But you're with the FBI now, right?"

"Yes," Allie said with a smile, knowing full well this woman had something important to add to the conversation. Who was she to stop her? "I work out of Quantico, but I'm just here on vacation. And you are?"

"Oh, I'm Stella Mayer. This is my husband, Chester." She leaned down until her upper body was practically laying across the table. She even held up her hand against her cheek, as if she was about to share trade secrets. "Chester doesn't believe me, but I keep hearing noises out in the backyard."

"Stella, I keep telling you that it's those darn raccoons rattling around in our barn. They're getting into the garbage cans, because you're not putting the lids back on tight enough." Chester shook his head in irritation, but it sounded as if this was an old argument that went back quite a long time. "Miss, I apologize. You're here on vacation and to spend time with your beau, Mitch. We shouldn't be talking out of turn about our raccoon problem."

"Mitch is doing a fine job as sheriff," Rose complimented, giving Allie an apologetic smile about the exchange between Chester and Stella. Allie found it sort of endearing that the two bantered back and forth over mundane things like garbage cans and could still love one another after most likely forty years of marriage bickering about animals digging through their trash. She'd seen the way Chester had snuck fries off Stella's plate. "We're lucky Mitch took over for Sheriff Percy. Now that man was just all wrong for the job."

"Don't you give that man such an honorable title. Percy doesn't deserve it, and he should have been run out of town on a rail after his role in Deputy Wallace's murder." Tiny rested his elbow on the table as he filled Allie in a little on the history of the two men. "I had to do my own law enforcement when it came to The Cavern. I ran that bar with an iron fist, and all because I didn't have a choice. Percy allowed almost every drunk in the neighborhood to play the friendship card, but that shouldn't have prevented the man from doing his job. Thankfully, Brynn has Lance, but also Sheriff Kendall to back them up. I knew Mitch from the time he sat on his mama's knee, and that boy has the courage it takes to do a damned fine job as our sheriff."

"Now you know as well as I do that Frank was devastated over Deputy Wallace's murder," Rose admonished with a wag of her finger. "Granted, he wasn't the best sheriff this town has ever seen, but he did view Deputy Wallace as a friend and solid member of the community."

"You're more forgiving then most, Rose."

"Wasn't Mr. Percy the sheriff back when Emma Irwin went missing?" Allie asked, believing she could stay in the diner all day to gather pertinent data to the case. These people were a wealth of information. "I guess he wasn't any better at his job earlier on in his career."

Tiny and Rose shared a knowing look with each other, and Chester was shaking his head as he took the last bite of his sandwich. Allie wasn't sure who the family was behind her, but they didn't seem inclined to join in on the discussion.

Sheriff Percy hadn't come up much in the case files that Mitch had sent Allie, but the way the investigation was handled back then played a big part in what law enforcement was dealing with now. Had Frank Percy purposefully mishandled evidence in the case to *help* out a friend? It was something that Thorne had more than likely already looked into, but it couldn't hurt to get someone else's opinion outside of the case.

The bell above the door jangled as someone entered the diner, and Allie didn't even have to look to know that it was Mitch. It had always been that way, but it was even more so now. Thankfully, his presence didn't deter Tiny from continuing his train of thought.

"I don't doubt that Frank Percy messed up that investigation from the second he'd declared Emma a runaway. If you ask me, the man knows exactly who has been terrorizing this town for so many years…and it's most likely one of his hunting buddies from across the lake. Most of those folks don't live here year-round like we do here in town. They have that snowbird mentality."

Allie wished she could have reassured Tiny and the rest of the patrons that he could have been onto something there, but that just wasn't the case. The killer they were looking for was definitely a local, and he could possibly be sharing a meal with them in this very diner.

CHAPTER FOURTEEN

"YOU LOOK LIKE you've been having fun," Mitch declared with a half-smile before reaching out and adjusting the light scarf that Allie had around her neck. Her cheeks were flushed from the cold November temperatures that had arrived with the start of the month, but her smile could brighten the darkest day even in gloomy weather. "What have you ladies been up to? I don't need to break out the handcuffs, do I?"

Two days had passed since he'd met up with Allie at the diner for lunch, only to find out that she'd already started her so-called undercover operation by chumming up to some of the locals. She'd done her best to blend in with the townsfolk, all on the basis of being more to him than an *old friend*.

She'd done a damn good job, too.

Mitch had known it would happen, but the lines had definitely been blurred into nonexistence. There wasn't a damned thing he could do about it now. Her cover was established.

"None of your business, Sheriff," Brynn answered for Allie with a laugh, looking both ways before she crossed the street with a quick wave. Dusk was falling, and her employees had covered the afternoon shift to give her a much-needed day off. "Let's just say you can thank us later."

Us must be in reference to Brynn, Shae, Reese, and Gwen. The four women had taken Allie on a tour of the shops on Main Street, no doubt stopping in at the woman's boutique next to the cleaners. Rumors had been spreading for days that the owner had received a shipment of sexy lingerie that should have gone to one of those adult stores in the city. From what he'd heard, sales were up tenfold.

The small discreet bag on Allie's arm was also a dead giveaway.

"Do I have to do something bad before you use those handcuffs on me, Ken?" Allie asked, lifting up on her tiptoes to give him a kiss on the lips for all to see. She then wrapped her arms around his neck and leaned in even closer to whisper in his ear. "Billy Stanton seems to be sans Julie tonight on his arm this evening, and he's walking our way."

Mitch was becoming rather adept at reading from the script, and he didn't hesitate to continue the show. His placation did not mean he was okay with this arrangement, which was the reason he'd called in reinforcements today that the feds wouldn't even know about unless needed. It was something he'd need to discuss with Allie, but now wasn't the time.

"Where are the other three deviants?" Mitch asked Allie, letting his voice carry so that Billy could easily hear their conversation as the man continued to walk toward them. Brynn had already jaywalked without a thought to who she'd been speaking to, leading the way for Mitch and Allie to follow. "Are they already inside The Cavern?"

"That's where the live entertainment is tonight, right?" Billy came to a stop beside them without his usual entourage. He had a smile pasted on his face, but Mitch wouldn't mind wiping it off if he got a chance. He restrained himself by taking ahold of Allie's hand and making sure she was on the other side of him. "Brynn certainly has changed the way this town parties on a Saturday night, hasn't she?"

"Brynn's a savvy business woman," Mitch praised, ignoring

the way Allie tightened her grip on his hand in warning. She was clearly telling him that she could take care of herself, but old habits die hard. He'd always protect the woman he was with, regardless that their public displays of affection were for show only. "Where's Julie tonight? I haven't seen her in a while."

"We're, uh, taking a break right now." Billy stepped off the curb rather quickly the minute Mitch mentioned Julie. His attempt at evading the topic was obvious. "How are things going with the case? It's all anyone's talking about for a week now."

Seeing as Mitch had been breathing and sleeping this investigation for much longer than that, he completely understood why everyone else was doing the same. These folks were on pins and needles, the press wanted answers on behalf of one of their own, and the feds were left tracking down every useless lead that was called in regarding the faintest bump in the night. Chester's raccoons had been investigated twice in the past week.

Law enforcement was basically running in circles.

"There's nothing new to report." Mitch thought back to how many times over the past week that he'd *accidentally* bumped into someone or purposefully cuffed their left shoulder during a discussion. No one had given any indication that they were recovering from the graze of a bullet. Unfortunately, Billy hadn't been one of those individuals. The distance between them was too far for Mitch to do anything about that now, but there would no doubt come a chance later this evening while they were all drinking at The Cavern. "The feds are still combing through several more recent leads, though."

Allie tugged Mitch's hand in an attempt to step out onto the street, as well. They really should have crossed at the intersection, even though traffic was extremely light at the moment. That would change within the hour as the Saturday night crowd gathered in the town's few hotspots.

"Billy, do you think your parents would sell one of those cottages they bought up at the lake?" Allie asked, purposefully standing her ground when Mitch attempted to get her to walk toward the intersection. "I was contemplating buying a place around here, but it seems that shell corporations are scooping up all the lakeside property the second it comes up for grabs."

"As I've said to several others earlier this week, I don't really talk to my parents about their side businesses." Billy shoved his hands into the pockets of his jacket. "You two enjoy your evening."

Mitch held Allie back from following their target across the street.

"Could we not instigate the situation until we've at least begun our evening?" Mitch had already looked into the connection between the Stanton family and the shell corporations that were currently buying up lakeside property. There was nothing illegal about what they were doing, and neither was anything wrong with Billy offering Noah a blank check for the Yoder farmhouse. "And before you ask, you can't just go up to Billy and punch him in the arm. That's not some kind of homespun greeting we do here."

"You can make damn sure I'm going to bump into him tonight," Allie promised, her penetrating brown eyes following her target's progress. "Billy Stanton danced with Emma Irwin at the bonfire the night she went missing. The bodies of those young girls were found at the bottom of the lake, which happens to surround the properties that the Stantons are purchasing at a rapid rate. Many of those lots aren't adjacent. What kind of value would they have if they aren't connected?"

"Harlan mentioned that sales have picked up this week, but I've known the Stantons a long time. They wait for the right moment to invest their money and jump on the armored truck and rake in the dividends." Mitch recognized Uncle Jimmy's truck and gave the man a wave, which was probably more than the man expected. When this investigation was all said and done, amends would need to be made. After all, family was still family and money shouldn't be enough reason to cause this much distance. The past would never be forgotten, but forgiveness was always on the table. "Let's head inside. It's getting colder out here by the minute, and Lance no doubt saved us one of the best tables in the place."

"Who was that man you just waved to?" Allie asked as she walked beside him across the street. Uncle Jimmy had pulled into the parking lot next to the bar, and Mitch was surprised when he didn't drive right back out. There must have been one spot left near the back, because the lot was jam-packed. "He looks familiar, but I don't recall seeing him this past week."

"That would be my uncle, Jimmy Webb. Our very own outcast of the clan—my mother's brother." Mitch didn't have to say anything more than that, because Allie had read the original crime reports. Uncle Jimmy had technically been the last to see Emma Irwin alive, claiming he'd seen her running down Seventh Street the night she'd been abducted. No one could verify his statement, and it hadn't helped that the man was an alcoholic who'd been drinking that very same night. "My mother and uncle had a strained relationship, so we're not exactly close."

"Agent Thorne documented in one of his reports that your uncle has never varied from his telling of the events that night." Allie stepped up on the sidewalk as she searched for the man in question. "My guess is that Jimmy Webb is telling the truth. He must have seen Emma that night on Seventh Street."

Mitch opened the door to the bar, allowing the country music blaring from the jukebox to spill out into the night. The live entertainment would be starting in around an hour, which would give Mitch a chance to get comfortable and survey the crowd while nursing a draft. Agent Thorne and Allie had secretly met and spent time constructing a list of suspects...and several of those individuals would be in attendance this evening.

"Sheriff!"

Damn it.

Just one night. Was that so hard to ask for? Mitch turned to find Byron walking down the sidewalk from the station. He'd been assigned to second shift, and there wasn't anything about this town that Deputy Warner couldn't handle, short of another abduction or homicide. Had anything new come up in the Blyth Lake killer case, Agent Thorne would have reached out to Mitch by cell phone.

"It's my night off, Warner." Mitch ushered Allie inside out of the cold, not wanting to linger outside any longer than necessary. "This better be good."

Mitch thought back to the conversation that Thorne and Allie had over the names that had been brought up in the twelve years that Emma had been missing. Byron was a part of that list, but he'd been brought up by two loving parents. He was content with his life, currently immersed in the dating scene, and in no other way fit the profile if one discarded his age.

"I thought you should know that the hospital called the station regarding Shelby Tilmadge, per your request." Byron motioned to the heavy wooden door still in Mitch's grasp. "I'm heading out that way now to make sure the press doesn't cause Shelby to have another mental breakdown. You know how he gets when there is too much activity on his property."

"I appreciate the heads up." Mitch didn't doubt that Byron had the experience to oversee the situation. He was a good deputy, followed the rules, and the residents of Blyth Lake trusted him. That trifecta went a long way in terms of keeping the peace in the surrounding neighborhoods. That didn't stop

Mitch from cuffing Byron on the left arm to give himself peace of mind. "Call Foster for backup if you run into any trouble, though I'm sure it's nothing you can't handle."

Byron nodded his appreciation for the vote of confidence before turning around and heading off to the SUV at a trot. Never once did the man wince or give any indication that he had any kind of wound on his upper arm.

"I saw that, Sheriff Kendall," Allie murmured, having stayed close by instead of entering the establishment. At least she hadn't called him Ken. He was still trying to break her of that habit outside of the bedroom. "I already told you that Byron isn't our unsub. Now watch closely."

Mitch would have ushered her back inside had she not stopped him, motioning for him to keep an eye on Byron as he waved to someone across the street. What had she picked up on that he hadn't?

"Byron Warner is left-handed. Our unsub is right-handed, with an injury to his left arm."

Mitch grit his teeth just enough to try and temper his frustration. He'd known that bit of information. Hell, he'd worked in close quarters with Bryon for some time now.

"He can shoot with both hands, unlike Deputy Foster."

"Has Byron given you any indication that he can't be trusted?" Allie asked, ignoring the calls for them to close the door. They'd been letting the cold air infiltrate the warm interior of the bar. She made it clear she wasn't going to move until he answered her question. "Is there anyone you do trust?"

"My family," Mitch replied without hesitation. He even went one step further, though he didn't understand why she appeared so shocked by his answer. After all, she was the one he'd called to save their asses from the darkness. "And you, Allie. I've always trust you."

CHAPTER FIFTEEN

ALLIE DIDN'T BELONG in a small town.

She needed bright lights, heavy traffic, strangers who didn't care about what she did or who she did it with, and a fucking Starbucks franchise.

Was that so much to ask for?

She wasn't cut out for complete strangers knowing her name, streets where no one cared if someone walked in front of them, and the random acts of kindness that weren't so random in a town like this.

Allie had quite a few close friends back in D.C. She wasn't hurting in that department, and she was rather tight with a couple of women in her apartment building. They had regularly scheduled evenings where they went to the local bar or dance club.

Granted, she no longer had any family in the area. Her father had passed away from complications arising from cirrhosis. That wasn't surprising given how much alcohol the man had drank, abusing his body right up to the end. They'd grown closer in his final year, but nothing could atone for the amount of parenting she'd missed out on while growing up without a mother.

"Mitch and Allie, I believe Lance reserved your family a table over by the dart boards," a man with white hair said as he took a seat next to a woman who was obviously his better half. Chester and Stella were also at the small table with a couple of pitchers of beer smack dab in the middle. "Hope you two enjoy your-selves tonight."

Allie rewarded everyone with a smile as she tried to quell the anxiety that was currently attempting to set up residence in her stomach. She didn't know what the hell was wrong with her, but maybe a shot of whiskey could temper her apprehensive nerves.

Mitch rested his hand on her lower back as he guided her through the crowded bar toward the back. Was it because he'd included her on his very short list of people he trusted? Of course, he trusted her. He never would have called in that favor if he hadn't.

"What's wrong?" Mitch asked with concern, leaning down so that only she could hear his question.

Allie made sure her smile stayed intact as she glanced up at him in reassurance. What could she say? That she was having a mini panic attack over the fact that the last four days had her questioning who she was as a woman?

She loved her life in D.C., and she would just have to remind herself of that every once in a while until she got back there.

"I need to use the restroom," Allie said, hoping a few minutes to herself would have her back in the saddle to do what needed to be done this evening. "Would you watch my bags and purse?"

"Has she got you tamed already, brother?" Lance laughed from the double tables he'd put together for their family. "I like your style, Allie."

Mitch immediately initiated the older brother routine, so she left the two alone to continue their sibling rivalry. She managed to cut through the large group next to the small hallway that led back to the restrooms. Someone mentioned the name Charlene Winston, but Allie couldn't hear the reply given by one of the other patrons. Everyone was talking over one another.

Finding the restroom empty was a huge relief, and Allie quietly closed the stall door behind her for even more privacy. She just needed a moment to herself to compose her wayward emotions. It was a good thing that Brynn kept The Cavern's restrooms clean and tidy. There was nothing worse than a nasty public toilet.

Allie breathed deeply, concentrating on the length of her inhalations and exhalations.

Nothing had changed.

She, Jay, his team of agents, and Mitch had all had a meeting at his house the other day to go over everything with a fine-tooth comb.

There had been no sign of Charlene Winston, the unsub had not reached out to any other news station, and all leads were proving to head nowhere. They were basically where they started, with the exception of Allie—who had spent days spreading breadcrumbs for the unsub.

Had she garnered his attention yet?

Would tonight be the night he came looking for her in the crowd?

Allie was mentally and physically prepared for anything thrown her way, though emotionally was a different matter altogether. And her conflicting emotions had nothing to do with the unsub or his motivations.

Her self-inflicted timeout had helped ground her, so Allie quickly utilized the restroom for its intended purposes. It wasn't long until she was drying her hands on a paper towel and opening the outer door to allow the country music to wash over her once more.

"Long time, no see," Reese said with a smile as she waited for Allie to step across the threshold. It didn't take long for her to realize that Reese hadn't needed to use the restroom at all.

"Jack and Beth Ann just announced that she's pregnant. He's at the far end of the bar buying drinks for anyone willing to cough up congratulations."

Allie didn't confirm nor deny that the information Reese had passed on was useful. What did she know, and more important-ly—how? Mitch would never have said a word to his family about the depth of the plan she and Jay had agreed upon. His discretion wasn't even in question.

Never once during the day that Allie had spent with the significant others of the Kendall brothers had they said anything about the case. Was Reese just assuming that Allie was still helping privately when it came to the profile?

Was Allie reading more into it than she should? Or had Noah and the rest of the family overheard something they shouldn't have in regard to Allie's presence?

"I don't know them very well, but I'm happy to hear the good news." Allie gently released the door and continued to walk into the throng of patrons. Regardless of the reason Reese had mentioned Jack and Beth Ann, it gave a solid excuse for Allie to accidentally bump into Jack. His back was toward her, which meant his left arm was wide open. "Oh, I'm sorry! It's so crowded in here that I—"

"No worries," Jack replied, reaching out to make sure she was okay. She didn't notice any sign of real pain, but he did hold his left arm close to his side afterward. Something was off in the manner in which he reacted. "Allie, have you met Beth Ann?"

"Hi," the redhead said with an infectious smile. She had a gorgeous glow about her that was perceptible. It was evident that she was ecstatic about the pregnancy, but would Jack step up to the plate? Allie had experienced firsthand the extent of his wandering eye, but he hadn't acted on it. At least, as far as she knew. Fatherhood might actually straighten his ass out. "I've heard so much about you! I work with Gwen over at her financial business a few blocks down, and she just adores you. She thinks you and Mitch are perfect for one another."

Allie refused to allow any guilt to overshadow tonight's agenda. She and Mitch had talked at length about his family and their involvement with this case. It was better they didn't know the depth of her participation, and that included Gwen.

"I can definitely say the same thing about her—she's a doll," Allie replied with a smile, ignoring the second statement entirely. She feigned a concerned look Jack's way. "Are you okay? I didn't mean to crash into you so hard."

"Oh, it's nothing. I pulled a rib muscle on the construction site last week."

"It actually bruised to the bone, can you believe that?" Beth Ann rubbed a hand up and down Jack's arm in comfort. "It's finally turned yellow as of this morning, so at least we know it's healing and he didn't break anything."

Allie had the information she needed, and Beth Ann had unknowingly just crossed Jack Stewart off the suspect list. If she'd seen his ribcage, then she'd seen the rest of his body. Everyone in Blyth Lake had heard about Gwen discharging her weapon and grazing the suspect's arm. Beth Ann didn't strike Allie as the type of woman to cover for a man who was capable of murdering over eighteen young girls and women.

"I should get back to the table," Allie replied with another apologetic smile. "You two enjoy your evening. Oh, and congratulations!"

She had maneuver around a few other people before she was able to walk a clear path to where Mitch was waiting for her. Lance and Noah were deep in conversation, while Jace and Shae must have arrived when Allie had been in the restroom.

"Allie, I stowed your belongings behind the bar," Lance said before sliding a cold bottle of beer her way. She was carrying, which meant she'd have no more than a couple of sips to have the others believe she was joining in the fun. "It's better to be safe than sorry."

"Thank you." Allie used the rung of the tall stool to hoist herself up into the seat, leaning against Mitch when he casually rested his arm on the back of her chair. She'd done so almost too naturally, but this had been the show they'd agreed to put on for the locals. Once everyone had gone back to their discussions, she leaned in so that only Mitch could hear her news. "Jack isn't our boy."

Mitch most likely would have questioned how she'd come by that intel, but Allie didn't want to go into a deep explanation with everyone around. Besides, it would also open up a can of worms regarding the issue of Reese knowing too much about Allie's role in the investigation.

The rest of the evening had been spent talking and laughing about everything but the case, which was a feat in and of itself. Allie kept a close eye on Billy, but there were a few other men at the bar who garnered her interest. Some were older than what her profile stated, but that had been known to happen. Maturity was a state of mind...not age.

Maybe Allie needed to be a little more vocal about her past.

"I'll grab the next round," Allie offered, hopping off the stool with a smile and hoping that no one noticed she was still nursing her first.

"There's no need for that," Mitch countered, his blue eyes not missing a thing. "Lance was about to—"

"I left my cell phone in my purse, and I really should check to see if I've got any messages." Allie wasn't going to delay the inevitable. She and Mitch had talked at length about what needed to take place. "I'll be right back."

Allie maneuvered through the crowd, stopping only long enough to say hello to those she personally met over the last four days. She spoke to Rose and Tiny the longest, giving her time to lay some more groundwork. Anyone overhearing them would know a little more about her upbringing.

"Allie, do you have any money left in that checking account of yours?" Gus asked with a knowing smile once Allie had slipped behind the bar. It was an odd angle to view everyone, but it showed her that Brynn or whoever was bartending could monitor just about every table in the joint. Interesting. "Word has it that Reese took you into the boutique."

"That she did," Allie laughed, leaning back enough so that she could see underneath the bar. Brynn's bartender, Kristen, was setting down two draft beers in front of Miles and another gentleman to his right. "And it wasn't just Reese's fault that my credit card almost caught on fire, but also Brynn, Shae, and Gwen. Those women are trouble with a capital T."

"I heard that," Brynn said good-naturedly as she walked back behind the bar. She whispered something to Kristen before kneeling to the floor. She stood back up with a smile, handing Allie her purse. "Is this what you're looking for?"

"Thanks, Brynn." Allie quickly checked her phone for messages, noting only one of significance. Jay had sent a text informing her that the hospital might have been too quick in releasing Shelby Tilmadge. There was no other explanation. "Is it okay if I still leave my purse back here? I'll take my cell phone with me."

"Sure thing."

Brynn was damned quick with her hands. She'd helped out Kristen by taking care of the patrons on this end of the bar. It was then that Allie realized Jeremy Bell wasn't in his usual spot.

Neither was Calvin, for that matter.

Mitch had mentioned something about a neighborhood watch at breakfast her first day in town. Were those two out and about on this cold night? Allie was now worried about them, considering their health was on the opposite side of vigorous.

"Brynn, do you know—"

"Giving up your fed job to be a small-town bartender?" Billy Stanton's question prevented Allie from asking Brynn about the whereabouts of her two usual patrons. Allie didn't miss the way Gus' fingers tightened on his beer mug. "Brynn, could we get another round of shots?"

"Sure thing, Billy."

Brynn gracefully reached for a handful of clean shot glasses lined up on the back shelf.

"I'd never make it as a bartender," Allie answered Billy's first question with a half-smile. He was one of those attention grabbers, but she'd found out the other day that he wasn't so keen on being on the receiving end of those jabs. She played it safe this time, hoping that he'd let his guard down just enough that she could take a peek underneath the surface. "I have a hard time keeping my opinions to myself."

Billy didn't banter back, which told her that he agreed with her deduction. Gus and Miles had a good chuckle at Billy's expense, though. Brynn muttered something good-natured under her breath that said she was opinionated herself, and that hadn't stop her from owning The Cavern.

It really was too bad that Allie wasn't on the other side of the bar. She'd already excluded Jack Stewart as the unsub, and she was hell bent on doing the same—or the opposite—with Billy Stanton.

"Allie, we have to go."

Mitch had suddenly appeared behind his father, his stern expression telling her that her plans might have to be put on hold. She didn't once question his reasoning, though, especially considering that he held her jacket in his hands. Whatever needed his attention was of a serious nature.

"Let me grab my things."

"Has something happened?" Gus asked with concern as Miles and the others all turned on their stools to hear Mitch's reply.

"Nothing that anyone needs to worry about tonight, Dad." Mitch had answered his father in the gentlest manner, but it was clear that something *had* taken place that needed the sheriff's immediate attention. "Are we meeting for breakfast in the morning?"

"Usual time, usual place," Gus replied, his lips thinning out as he then quietly looked on as Allie finished gathering her bags. She really had spent quite a bit of change today. "Be careful out there, son."

Allie gave Brynn and the other bartender an apologetic smile as she carefully maneuvered herself out from behind the bar. Mitch met her halfway, though that took her farther away from her target. There was no elegant manner in which she could accidentally bump into Billy Stanton without alerting him and others to her intent.

She'd have to wait for another opportunity to present itself.

Allie remained silent as Mitch led her through the crowded bar of those waiting for the live entertainment to begin their first music set. It wasn't until they were outside of the establishment that he motioned for her to put the bags down on the sidewalk so that he could help her into her jacket.

"The body of a female was recovered on the side of the road around ten miles outside of town." Mitch leaned down and grabbed her shopping bags only after she'd buttoned her dress coat. He didn't waste time crossing the street nor giving her the specific detail that had captured his attention. "The victim had red hair, Allie. Our plan may have very well backfired and gotten Charlene Winston killed."

CHAPTER SIXTEEN

"**I** DON'T BELIEVE the hit and run has anything to do with our case."

"I agree with you, but that still leaves us with no leads to pursue," Mitch countered as he poured himself a fresh cup of coffee. Monday wasn't shaping up to have the best morning. "Speaking of the hit and run, have the state police made any progress on an ID?"

The hit and run on the female that had taken place on Saturday night had been outside of town and in the jurisdiction of the state police. The tragic accident had nothing to do with the serial killer investigation, but the woman's death still mattered to her loved ones left behind.

In the end, the outcome of the hit and run meant that there was a slim chance Charlene Winston could still be alive.

Mitch and Allie had decided to drive home instead of returning to The Cavern. She'd gone into detail about her *accidental* run-ins with some of the male individuals on the suspect list, but she revealed she hadn't been able to do the same with Billy.

Was Billy Stanton their unsub?

"I haven't heard from the state investigator this morning, but the woman's clothes revealed what color paint was on the vehicle. That might help them in solving the case." Thorne tossed down one of the many manila folders that were now scattered across the table. He rested his head back against the chair and closed his eyes. It just went to show that hardly any of them were getting the rest they needed. "It's nearly been a week since Charlene Winston was taken from the inn."

"Time is running out for her, if it hasn't already." Mitch didn't bother to go back into his office. Byron was patrolling the neighborhoods and taking the calls that needed immediate attention from the sheriff's department. Deputy Foster had been scheduled for second shift. The new hire would be on thirds for quite a few months before Mitch would rotate him out with Foster. "We may have to face the fact that we played this entire situation wrong."

Mitch's opinion garnered Thorne's attention. The agent sat up in his seat and took a good look around the station. The only one who could possibly overhear them at the moment was Patty, but she was busy reassuring one of the locals that Raymond Dixon was well aware there was a hole in the fence on the east side of his property.

"We didn't play this wrong, Mitch." Thorne went searching for a particular file. Once it was in his hand, he then tossed it across the table. "Agent Stringer agreed with Allie's assessment of the unsub. Her presence in town will capture this son of a bitch's attention. He's a smart one, and I don't believe he's going to act on impulse. It's just a matter of when he decides to act, and you're not going to like what I have to say."

"Allie has already gone around town to almost every shop, spreading her story of an unhappy childhood in her wake. There isn't anything else she could do besides hold up a sign with a red bullseye."

Mitch didn't have the stomach for his second cup of coffee. The first one he'd shared with Allie while they sat on the porch and watched the sun rise. He was getting used to having her there to talk to every day, and that would eventually become a problem. Hell, it already was a problem.

"What if there was a way we could—"

"Mitch, Byron just radioed in. He's over with Lester Feen, who's been complaining about Raymond Dixon's fence line having holes on the east side." Patty was tapping a pencil against her hand, and she only ever did that when something was more wrong than usual. "Byron's requesting both you and Agent Thorne head out that way to have a look at these so-called holes in the ground. Something odd is going on."

Mitch didn't hesitate. He pushed back the chair, stood before taking his keys out of the front pocket of his jeans, and then started for the front door. Thorne followed closely behind him after having grabbed his suit jacket.

"I'll drive."

Mitch had left his lightweight jacket in the sheriff's vehicle. He knew exactly where the east side of Dixon's farm was located, and it was a bit of a hike.

"You want to tell me who the hell Raymond Dixon is and why he'd have multiple holes dug on his property?" Thorne snapped his fingers as he reached for the handle on the passenger side door. "Wait. Dixon. I came across that surname when I was looking into the Emma Irwin's files."

"Raymond Dixon is the son of Stanley and Birdie. Stanley died a very long time ago, but Birdie was the woman who ran the camp that Emma Irwin and Sophia Morton attended the summer before Emma went missing." Mitch yanked on the driver's side door handle. Raymond technically fit the profile, if age wasn't a factor. Had lady luck finally made an appearance? "Thorne, we might just have the break we've been looking for."

"I'M SURPRISED YOU don't own one of the cottages," Allie told

Brynn as they walked along the sand by the lake. The sky was overcast and the wind was quite cold, both ingredients causing the day to seem quite dreary. The large body of water should have held a peaceful quality, but it had been taken the moment evil had dipped its toe in the gentle wind-driven current. "You bought The Cavern from Tiny and Rose, right?"

"I did, but Tiny and Rose had grand thoughts about overdue vacations." Brynn leaned down and picked up a straw wrapper that had somehow been left behind. She stowed the litter in the pocket of her black coat. "Rose was very close to Birdie Dixon back in the day. A lot of the camp's lake property was sold to Rose after Birdie passed, because Raymond Dixon had no interest in taking over the camp or running that kind of business. Let's face it, the restaurant and the beach area take a lot of work all by themselves."

"But Tiny and Rose were hoping that the off season would allow them to travel," Allie surmised as she swept her gaze over the small pier. No boats were currently moored to the wooden deck. "I'm sorry this all happened to you."

"There's only one person to blame." Brynn tucked a blonde lock of hair behind her ear as the wind picked up. "Reese, Shae, and I know what you're up to, Allie. You really need to be more careful. Truthfully, we're all surprised that Mitch is allowing you to act as bait for this guy. He's dangerous, he's smart, and he's capable of catching you by surprise."

This was one of the reasons Allie had wanted to spend time with Brynn. What had Allie or Mitch done to give themselves away? If the women were aware of Allie's attempt to lure in the unsub, then it was possible that the unsub was aware, too.

It was Monday afternoon, which meant Reese and Shae would be at work. Brynn technically should be at the bar getting ready for the evening crowd, but she'd handed over the reins to

Kristen after Allie had made the request.

"Why would you believe I'm offering myself up for bait?"

Allie saw a bench in the distance, though her attention was still on the parking lot up and over the hill. They were now too far away to see any vehicles coming or going. The sense that someone was watching her had begun earlier this morning when she'd met Gus for breakfast. Unfortunately, she hadn't been able to pinpoint the source.

"Really?" Brynn laughed and shook her head at Allie's question. "Come on. Tell me the truth. You grew up in some posh suburb on the East Coast with two loving parents, maybe a brother or two in light of how well you handle the Kendall men, and a white picket fence. There is no way you fit the profile—no pun intended—of the serial killer who's been hunting young girls in Blyth Lake. You're not the type."

Allie wished more than anything she could tell Brynn that her fairytale of a childhood was accurate. Unfortunately, that wasn't the case. The silver lining in all of this was that if the unsub thought it was all a fake story, he could easily pull up some articles online which covered her past since she'd joined the service and then the FBI.

She'd made the paper a time or two in regard to some high-profile cases, and the military was fond of doing hometown press releases every time someone got promoted, received a commendation, or graduated from a training course. It was amazing the depths a reporter would go to for a compelling story.

"Brynn, my past isn't some cover that Mitch and I came up with in order to lure this unsub out of hiding." They'd made it to the bench, and Allie was the first to take a seat. She might as well get comfortable and explain her history. "Unfortunately, I didn't have the perfect childhood you and the girls imagined. It's true that I grew up with an alcoholic father and no mother. It's also a cold hard fact that I joined the military to escape a dead-end road that I was going to find myself on if I'd stayed at home. In reality, being a Marine saved my life."

Brynn studied Allie for a good thirty seconds before replying, most likely to gauge the sincerity of her story.

"Allie, I'm so sorry. We didn't mean to—"

"It's okay." And it was okay. Allie had made peace with her past a long time ago, though she was beginning to doubt herself in that area. She'd be fine once she made it back to D.C. "I can see how you and the others would think Mitch and I had made up some story to aid the investigation, but my childhood wasn't the greatest."

Allie didn't allow guilt to wash over her at the fact she'd stretched the truth a little. The unsub had been too quiet since Thorne had released the personal background of Charlene Winston. Had the reporter been killed? Had the unsub taken another life outside of his unspoken code in his attempt at giving his victims peace?

"We have a lot more in common than you think, Brynn."

Allie casually looked over her shoulder, but she didn't have a line of sight to the parking lot any more than when she'd been three feet away from the bench. Was her imagination working overtime? It was doubtful, given the circumstances.

"You're wondering why the killer hasn't targeted me." Brynn crossed her arms as she focused on something out in the water. "I mean, I lost both of my parents. I was a little hellion back in the day, and I certainly gave Rose and Tiny a run for their money."

Allie had already put two and two together. Rose and Tiny were the reason Brynn had never been chosen to join the other young girls in their new home. She'd inadvertently gotten her own family who'd stepped in to raise her, nurture her, and love her.

"You're very lucky to have Rose and Tiny," Allie said softly before breathing in the lake air, the crisp scent warning them that winter was just days or maybe a few weeks away. "Have you considered—"

"If you're not working this investigation the way we all thought, what is going on between you and Mitch?"

Allie had been trying to steer the conversation in the direction of Brynn's role in town. Owning The Cavern put her in direct line of every single resident who graced the doors to the bar. The way rumors spread and the manner in which the townsfolk talked over a beer or two, important information must have been said at one time or another. It was just a matter of remembering.

It appeared that particular discussion was tabled until Allie answered a few questions of her own.

Honestly, she should have seen this coming.

"Mitch and I are…" Allie waved her hand in hopes that words would magically appear before her, but that didn't happen. Damn it. "It's complicated."

Allie liked it better when she could blame the tequila.

"I don't believe there's been a relationship in existence that wasn't complicated."

"Mitch and I have been friends for a very long time. We, uh…well, we inadvertently crossed that line around a year ago." Allie shuffled her feet and leaned forward on the bench a bit. She was a profiler, for fuck's sake. She should be able to redirect this conversation in a matter of seconds. "We corrected our mistake, he reached out to me to call in a chip, and I came here to help out if I can."

Brynn continued to study Allie. The roles should have been

reversed, and she realized just how far this conversation had gotten carried away from her. She cleared her throat and tried once more to take back the reins of this conversation.

"The line has disappeared again, but it will be back in place before I leave for D.C."

"Not home?"

Allie shot Brynn a look, wondering how she could have missed her previous declaration.

"Yes, back to D.C."

"You don't call D.C. your home, other than to reference your childhood. You always call the city by its name."

"Are you sure you're Brynn and not Shae?" Shae was the psychiatrist, but a bartender came damn close. "I get it, Brynn. You're concerned about Mitch. You don't need to be."

"We all are," Brynn replied with a small smile. "Mitch is what holds the Kendall clan together. He's the glue that keeps the family bond intact the way Mary would have wanted it, and no one wants to see him get hurt."

So, this was the reason that it hadn't been hard to pry Brynn away from The Cavern.

"We both are well aware of what happens at the end of my two weeks' vacation."

Right?

Allie's entire life was back in D.C. She'd be a fool to walk away from her job in the Bureau. It wasn't like Mitch had asked her to, anyway.

Thinking back over her career, maybe this was why Allie didn't take vacations. Time away from work made a person reevaluate his or her life. She didn't need to do that, because being a profiler was all she'd ever wanted.

"You came here to spend your vacation with Mitch and give him advice on the profile of a serial killer," Brynn surmised, crossing her ankles in an effort to capture some heat. It really was getting quite cold sitting here on the bench in front of the water. "That must have been one hell of a favor you owed him."

Allie relaxed somewhat as cherished memories from her past began to surface.

"Oh, you don't know the half of it," Allie laughed with a shake of her head. She was glad she'd left her hair down so that the heavy strands covered her ears. A hat would have been more preferable, but she figured they'd start to walk back to their vehicle shortly. One more story, and then they could begin to head back. She really would love to take another look at the vehicles in the parking lot. "Mitch covered for my ass after our CO—that's the Commanding Officer of our unit—caught me sneaking into the officer's club supply tent to steal a bottle of booze. You see, while on deployment, only officers have access to hard liquor in the field. That is, if you don't manage to pack it in yourself."

Allie can still remember the fear that shot through her at being caught red-handed. She'd pretty much done things by the book from that moment on, with very few exceptions. This case being one of them.

"Mitch is a good man, Brynn. I'm glad I was able to spend this time with him, as well as give my two cents worth on this investigation. It's clear that he feels responsible for this town."

"Blyth Lake represents Mary Kendall in every way that counts, and Mitch wants to protect that legacy." Brynn shot Allie another glance, this time with mischief in her eyes. "It might only be for another week, but we're all glad that he has you by his side right now. He's not nearly as edgy as he was before you arrived."

"Edgy?" Allie let loose another laugh, knowing exactly what Brynn meant about the manner in which Mitch carried himself.

"There were quite a lot of adjectives we all used to describe Mitch back in the day, and edgy is being polite. I'll add it to the list, though."

"I really should be heading back," Brynn said reluctantly before pushing to her feet. "What are you going to do for the rest of the day, Miss I'm Just Vacationing? Word has it that Agent Thorne doesn't want you in the station."

"Agent Thorne is just doing the job he was hired to do," Allie countered, not stating anything that wasn't fact. They were purposefully keeping the status quo, because it was just a matter of time before the unsub made a move against her. If the day came when she was supposed to return to the city that action hadn't been taken against her, those involved with the investigation would come up with an excuse as to why she was extending her time here. She was hoping it wouldn't come to that...for several reasons. "I'll just head back to The Cavern with you, if that's okay. I'd like to ask you some questions about the night Emma Irwin was taken. It might help me round the corners on the profile I crafted for Mitch. And it will give me something to do until he gets off his shift later."

The sheriff's position was technically a twenty-four-hour job, but Brynn understood what Allie meant in the broad spectrum of the workday. She fell in step as they both headed back down the sandy beach to where the stairs led up to the parking lot above.

"Of course, but I'm pretty sure I answered every question that was asked over the last twelve years," Bryn answered wryly. She shoved her hands in her jacket now that they were walking into the wind. "Ask away."

Allie, Mitch, and Jay had sat for hours the other day poring over the interviews that had taken place back then and now. Frank Percy had covered the ground pretty well, given that he hadn't been all that proficient at his job. There had been one specific question that hadn't been asked by either Frank Percy or Detective Kinkaid.

"We all know who was at the bonfire that night," Allie said, holding out hope that this new direction might poke a hole in the darkness that cloaked this case and let in a bit of sunshine. "Who wasn't in attendance that night who you believe should have been there, Brynn? Who was missing?"

CHAPTER SEVENTEEN

"COME BACK TO bed."

Mitch couldn't stop his lips from forming a smile, even though Allie couldn't see his reaction as he continued to sit on the couch. He'd heard her light footsteps coming down the stairs. It was a comforting sound that had him reevaluating this past week, but now wasn't the time to talk about the change in their relationship status.

He leaned back against the cushions, having been hunched over various witness statements for hours. The dull, constant ache in his hip didn't help matters, either.

"I couldn't sleep." Mitch held up his hand, loving the feel of hers as she locked her fingers with his. She came around the left side of the couch, never once breaking contact with him. "Hey, I spilled coffee on that shirt."

Mitch was usually quite neat when it came to his home. That being said, he'd grown used to having her there to come home to every night for a week. He'd gotten into the bad habit of letting his clothes hit the ground while being distracted by her tantalizing beauty.

"Ask me if I care that it smells of coffee and you." Allie had taken a seat next to him, but she'd swung her legs over his lap. He held them against his chest so that she didn't get chilly. He'd had to turn the furnace on with this cold front that had come through after the holiday. "I love your cologne."

Mitch caught himself just in time. He'd been going to say *more than me*, but it would have caused an uncomfortable rift between them that he couldn't deal with right now.

"I know you're concerned about the gravesite you found on Raymond Dixon's farm, but I don't believe he's our unsub."

"That leaves us back at square one." Mitch gestured toward the numerous files in front of him. "You and I both know this son of a bitch is to blame for those two graves. And now that Lester Feen has basically announced to the entire town that he found two open body-sized holes in the ground, we've had to settle for a few discreetly placed trail cameras and foot patrols at random intervals instead of leaving an officer to monitor the area."

"Even though it is unlikely the unsub will return, Jay will still have someone surveying the area for activity using those cameras. I bet we'll catch at least a few media types snooping around up there. It might be a waste of time, but it's protocol. Who knows, we might get lucky. Maybe the unsub didn't hear the latest news circulating The Cavern." Allie rested an elbow on the back of the couch, but her graceful movement appeared almost too calculated. Something was up, and she now had him on edge. "The unsub hasn't used the graves yet. That tells me that there's still a chance that Charlene Winston is alive. He could be holding her someplace as a prisoner until he figures out how to dispose of her without violating his code."

Allie was still keeping something from him. He'd known her for a very long time. There wasn't a sentence that came out of her mouth that hadn't been run through that brain of hers twice over.

"Thorne was thinking about stopping by in the morning to run a few scenarios by you, barring nothing else happens by zero seven hundred."

"Really?" Allie's brown eyes was taking in every expression that crossed his face. He braced himself once he recognized the drip of sarcasm from her one word inquiry. "Are you also going to invite the two men who have been monitoring my every move today?"

Damn it all to hell.

"You do realize that I could have been arrested for murder had I done a little hunting of my own?" Allie wasn't going to cut him any breaks, and she had every right to be pissed. "I can't believe you brought Chaz and Deet in on this. What were you thinking, Ken?"

Mitch had been contrite until she'd used his nickname.

"I was thinking that Thorne has enough to deal with, and that you need someone watching your back twenty-four-seven." Mitch removed her legs from his lap so that he could stand. His defenses had been breached. He knew it, she knew it, but he'd made the decision all the same. "How the hell did you make them? They haven't set foot inside town."

"No, they haven't made that mistake. Yet. And it wasn't until Brynn and I drove up to the lake that I thought I'd caught sight of a vehicle tailing us a couple hundred yards back." Allie lowered her hand from the back of the couch, wrapping her arms around her legs as she got comfortable. This meant they were a long way from returning to that warm bed upstairs, but he had no one to blame but himself. "Does Thorne know you brought in mercs from the outside?"

"No, and I wouldn't call them mercenaries...at least, not to their face." Mitch debated on leaving his answer at that, but he could easily sense the anger ratcheting up in this situation. He would still make the same decision if he had to do it all over again. "Who sets up this type of sting without surveillance, Allie? No one. And I don't like that Thorne is playing this part of the investigation so loose. You're a viable target, and it's only a matter of time before the unsub makes contact with you to judge your viability for himself."

"And when have I ever been alone?" Allie pointed out one of the rules she and Thorne had gone over numerous times. If the unsub saw that she was being guarded, their plan would be for naught. Mitch got that, but he didn't have to like it. She uncurled herself from the couch, giving him a glimpse to the fact that she wore nothing underneath his t-shirt. He'd like nothing better than to take her back upstairs, but she was just getting started as she lifted a hand to use her fingers in listing off the procedures they'd all put in place. "I never go anywhere alone. I always carry my cell phone with me, which allows Thorne to see my every move. I check in on the hour, every hour. And my nights are spent here with you, with a fucking grade-A alarm system that's better than the one on my office at Quantico. No one can get to me, let alone the unsub."

"Don't even go there, Allie." Mitch had been right to call in Chaz and Deet. They were professionals who easily equaled anybody Thorne could have selected from his own Hostage Recovery Team division. She was about to go off half-cocked, and Thorne was so far at the end of the rope that the man might actually go along with whatever she'd concocted in that head of hers. "First off, the plan we have in place certainly isn't fool-proof. There are a million ways the unsub can reach you, especially if he's someone we all trust."

"You don't trust Billy Stanton."

"No, but he has never been—"

Mitch was beginning to hate that she had such intelligence to weed out the useless facts of a case within days. No one trusted Billy. Emma might have trusted him back in high school, but opinions had changed over the years.

"So, you're ruling out Billy?" Mitch asked warily, knowing full well he wasn't off the hook about the whole Chaz and Deet caper. "Is that wise? He fits the profile in almost every way. He also had the chance to take Emma the night she went missing. Everyone at that bonfire said it wasn't five minutes after Emma left for home that everyone else began to disperse due to the incoming storm. Every young male at that party had ample time to abduct her before she made it out of the woods."

"I asked Brynn a question today that I believe holds some merit, and it was a question no one has thought to ask her up to this point." Allie leaned down and began to search through the files, and it didn't take her long to find the one she wanted. He always did like a specific logical order when it came to working a case, and it appeared she'd caught onto his precision rather quickly. "Who wasn't at the bonfire who should have been there? Someone who everyone expected to see that night, but didn't."

It was an angle that could easily be looked at in depth, though it would require some time. Granted, their high school didn't hold the number of graduates that others outside of Blyth Lake had in comparison. It still made for a long night.

"You need to call off Chaz and Deet. Put them on call, if you'd like. But pull them for now." Allie shook her head when Mitch went to argue, giving him the very reasons why it had been a bad idea to begin with. "They're going to get caught by someone, most likely by one of the agents working the case with Jay. Either that or one of the locals will take matters into their own hands when they find out that Chaz and Deet are using their deer stands. They're using them in the fields to give them a vantage spot so Deet can use those fancy pair of tactical binoculars he's is so fond of. You're going to blow my cover, Mitch, and then we're going to lose the only shot we've been given."

Mitch couldn't counter her logic. He tried to come up with any precaution that would keep her marginally safer, given the situation. Unfortunately, he was at a complete loss. The damnedest part of what they were facing landed at his feet. He was responsible for putting her in front of the son of a bitch who'd spent most of his adult life killing young women for the sole purpose of establishing a bond with his victims.

"I'll be fine, Ken." Allie gradually closed the distance between them before wrapping her arms around his waist. She tilted her head back when he sighed in agreement. "It's not that I don't appreciate you wanting to keep me safe. I do, but this is part of my job. I know how to protect myself."

"And what if it wasn't part of your job? What if you didn't work for the FBI anymore?" Mitch had always been a man who was upfront about everything in his life. Honesty made the days easier, and it sure as hell helped him sleep better at night. There was no need to hedge his bet when he spoke the truth. "What if we made a mistake by walking away from each other a year ago?"

Allie slowly released her hold on him until she was able to step back, giving her the space that she obviously needed to collect herself. He had to curl his fingers into the palms of his hands to keep from reaching out to her.

"We didn't."

"How can you be so sure?"

Mitch took in every fleeting expression that crossed her beautiful face. She appeared scared. When he'd walked away from her in D.C., it had been because of personal shit that he hadn't been able to put in its rightful place back then. He'd rectified that, and he now had a home. A home with a front door that he was ready to open in order to finally allow other people to walk into his life.

"Allie, our lives are in different places now than they were a year ago."

"For you, maybe. Not me." Allie reached back and grabbed her hair, pulling the heavy strands off her shoulders. She always kept it secured at the base of her neck when working. He'd always believed it was a habit left over from her days in the Corps, but he was quickly realizing that it was a part of her battle armor. "I still have my life back in the city, and I sure as hell am not cut out for the kind of commitment you're talking about. I never have been, because I'm too focused on my job to have time for a family. That's not likely to change any time soon. You're also forgetting that we both agreed things would go back to normal once this case was solved. I need to know I can still count on you to honor our agreement, Mitch."

There was a bit of desperation in her tone that told him she didn't believe in her own stance. He could also sense that now wasn't the time to push her into a conversation about their relationship. It was best that things remain status quo until she was out of the crosshairs of the serial killer they were attempting to draw out of hiding. He didn't like postponing the inevitable, but she didn't need the additional stress at this point in the investigation.

"You'll always be able to count on my word, Allie," Mitch quietly reassured her, opening his arms and hoping that she didn't pull away from him completely. He breathed a sigh of relief when she tentatively stepped back into his embrace. He held her close to his chest, inhaling her sweet scent and savoring this moment with her that could end all too soon. "I think I'm ready to get some rest now."

"Good," Allie whispered, though her sentiment was muffled against his chest. "It was getting cold up there without you."

"We can't have you getting a chill," Mitch murmured against her hair. He leaned down so that he could press his lips against her neck. Yes, he needed to live in the moment and try to push the worry about tomorrow to the side…for now. "I believe I know a way to make you very, very hot, Special Agent Delaney."

"I like the sound of that." Allie took him by the hand and guided him past the couch, though she did stop long enough to swipe his cell phone off the cushion. She gave him a knowing smile and wiggled the device in her fingers. "You can give Chaz and Deet a call before warming up my engine, Ken. I know how fond you are of those loose ends."

That was one of the small issues when getting involved with a good friend—Allie could play him like a fiddle. Well, two could play at that game. Unfortunately, it wasn't his turn. Nor was it hers. The initiative lay solely at the feet of a killer, and it was only a matter of time before he decided to roll the dice.

CHAPTER EIGHTEEN

FOUR MORE UNEVENTFUL, long drawn-out days had passed without the unsub making a move of any kind.

Allie was both troubled by the quiet, but also quite thankful for the additional time she'd been granted with Mitch. He'd messed with her head when he suggested that they hadn't made a mistake in crossing that blurred line for the first time a year ago. The only good thing to come from their talk was that he'd called off Chaz and Deet. Sending them home was for the best.

Truthfully, she hadn't seen them in years. It would have been nice to get some of the old gang together, but it was paramount for everyone involved that they keep their distance. They could make up for lost time later, after the case was closed.

As it stood, it was Friday morning and the sun still hadn't been allowed to come out to play. Dark clouds hung overhead, as if they hadn't decided whether to unleash a cold rain or surprise everyone with the season's first snowfall.

Personally, Allie voted for a bit of flurries. She'd never been a huge fan of the holidays, but she did hum along with a few Christmas carols every now and then when the mood struck her. She'd always opted to work Thanksgiving and Christmas, giving those family men and women the chance to spend it with their loved ones.

Taking a vacation this late in the year would definitely see her on rotation for those two holidays, as well as New Years.

"Did you stop by just to get a cappuccino? I should take offense to that, but I fully understand the withdrawal you must be going through," Gwen said good-naturedly, tapping something into her keyboard before swinging her chair around. She looked great compared to the last time Allie had seen her, with a flush in her cheeks and a smile on her face. "Come on. I'll join you for a double-shot espresso with cream."

"You relax. I'll grab us those two cups of sanity," Allie suggested, not wanting to waste any more time than needed. She was technically supposed to go back to D.C. on Sunday, but that wasn't likely to happen without the unsub making his move. It was time to think about how she and Mitch were going to spin their next story. Jay already had things covered with Allie's Supervisory Agent back at Quantico. "There's something I was hoping to discuss with you in private."

Allie didn't have to point out that Beth Ann would be able to hear every word that was said if they talked by the coffee station. Even though Jack had been virtually removed from the suspect list, one could never be too careful. It wouldn't do to have Beth Ann overhear Allie asking Gwen about the nightmares she'd been having regarding the night of her attack.

It didn't take Allie long to use the cappuccino machine after removing her insulated jacket. She had an appliance similar to this one in her apartment, and her mouth was drooling by the time she'd got done brewing the makings for two cups, and adding a dollop of cream while topping them off with just the right amount of foam.

"I can't believe I haven't been into your office earlier." Allie closed the office door with her foot, hoping that Beth Ann would think it a natural move to do when entering someone's private domain. "The first day I arrived, Molly mentioned you having the machine of all machines for those *fancy* coffee drinks."

"How do you think I lure my clients here?" Gwen slid her cup closer, inhaling the delicious aroma as she closed her eyes to savor the delectable scent. "Mmmm…works like a charm."

Allie was too busy relishing the hot beverage as it hit the back of her tongue. It showed Mitch's true talent when it came to distracting a woman, because it was hard to believe that she'd forgotten her love of a good double.

Score one for going back to D.C.

"I hear we owe you an apology." Gwen sat back in her chair, her blue eyes focusing on Allie much like Mitch did when trying to size someone up. "Brynn mentioned your conversation from the other day and that we misjudged the situation substantially."

"Why do I feel I'm about to get a warning of some sort?" Allie asked, not surprised that Gwen would issue a cautionary threat when it came to her older brother. Mitch and Gwen had a very strong bond, and it must be killing Mitch to keep her and his brothers in the dark. "Gwen, it's not my intention to do any harm to your brother. We've been friends for a very long time, and our relationship has…grown. I still plan to go back to my life in D.C."

"That's what worries me," Gwen responded with genuine concern. She sat forward in her chair and rested her elbows on her desk. "I'm sure your intentions are pure, Allie, but I see the way Mitch looks at you. More so as each day passes that we have you here in town."

Gwen held up her hand when Allie would have argued against that opinion. This wasn't how this morning's meeting was supposed to go. It seemed to be running off the rails right now without a handle to pull.

"I know why Mitch brought you to town. I realize that you can help with the profile, and that maybe you'll be able to point

Mitch in the right direction. What neither one of you have recognized is the fact that you've blended into our family as if you're one of us." Gwen rested her hands on the desk as she drove home her point, which was honestly causing Allie a bit of nausea. "I personally would love the relationship between you and Mitch to work out. He truly deserves happiness, and I've gotten to see his eyes sparkle these past two weeks. I'd hate to see you extinguish that light."

Allie didn't think it was possible, but she was no longer in the mood for the double espresso in her hands. She carefully set the cup on the edge of the desk, debating if she shouldn't just leave without getting the answers she'd come here for.

Gwen was protecting her brother. Allie understood that, and she even appreciated that Mitch had such a loving family. They were the reason he'd returned to Blyth Lake, and it was easy to see that the Kendall family was stronger as a unit than they were apart.

"I'm sorry, Allie. I didn't mean—"

"Yes, you did." Allie gave Gwen a small smile of regret. "I wish I could tell you that Mitch and I aren't going to hurt one another, but I can't give you that kind of guarantee. I will say that I've got a horrible track record when it comes to relationships, but your brother has a way about him that makes him hard to resist. My life is in D.C., and I plan to go back after—"

Allie almost slipped, but she'd caught herself just in time.

"I plan to go back to the city after this weekend." Allie cleared her throat and decided to get the information she came for before walking down to the diner. She wouldn't technically be alone, but it would give the patrons a chance to see that she didn't always have someone directly by her side. "Seeing as Mitch has a case to oversee, I was hoping to finish my profile for him. You know, to pay back that favor I owe him. It's technically the reason I'm here in the first place, and I'd hate to leave town without giving him what I'd promised to provide."

Gwen appeared to want to walk back some of the discussion they'd stumbled over when it came to Mitch and Allie's personal life. It was a relief when his sister nodded her agreement to the change in topic altogether.

"What is it that I can help you with, Allie?"

"Mitch mentioned that you were having nightmares about your attack. I was hoping that maybe there were some details of that night that were coming back to you."

Allie searched Gwen's face for any sign that she recalled something new. It was a long shot, and Gwen would have told Mitch first thing, but there were times another perspective could jog the memory.

"I've gone over every minute of my attack a number of times," Gwen revealed, sitting back in her chair. She glanced out the window to where Beth Ann sat at her desk. "Do you know the depths this scumbag had to have gone through in order to make sure every event happened exactly as he needed it to in order to get me alone at the house without electricity?"

"Mitch explained that Chad had spent the day with his family attending an annual remembrance ceremony for their mother, but that he and his father had been run off the road on their way back to Blyth Lake." Allie had gone over Gwen's statement numerous times, and she became more confused with each read through. "You also spent the day with your family, and Irish was the one who dropped by Gus' place to inform you that Chad needed a tow back to town after running his truck into a ditch."

"Yes, Irish drove out to Dad's place to tell me what was going on." Gwen looked down at her double espresso, pausing long enough in her story to take another sip. Allie was still quite nauseous, so she refrained from picking up her cup again.

"When I drove home, the house was dark. I mean, completely dark due to the power being out. There was no electricity to the property, which meant my security system wasn't up and running. Nor were the cameras."

"But you didn't go inside right away." Allie threw out a few facts to keep Gwen on target. Jogging the memory could be very successful in recalling details that were missed the first time around. "You called Mitch first, right?"

"Yes." Gwen took another sip of her espresso, but she was frowning by the time she'd set the cup back down. "We came to realize later that the sick fuck had actually gone to drastic lengths in causing Chester and Stella to have the accident that plunged half the town into a blackout that night. It's the only reason I parked my Jeep and went into the house."

"The unsub lured you into believing it was safe to go inside, believing everyone in town was dealing with the same electrical outage and that it wasn't related to the unsub's actions." Allie wasn't surprised at how far the individual they were searching for would go in order to get what he wanted, but he'd done something he hadn't before—put people he respected in harm's way. Unless his respect for them had been damaged by their reactions to the media's coverage. Was the unsub unraveling? "Gwen, what were Chester and Stella doing that Sunday evening?"

"They have a standing double date with Harlan and his wife every Sunday night." Gwen shook her head with a sad smile. "And yes, Mitch and I have gone over that situation numerous times. Everyone in town is well aware of those couples getting together every Sunday night, in addition to their scheduled game nights."

"Gwen, did you recognize your attacker?"

Allie had waited to ask the question until Gwen was deep

into her recollection of that night. In her profession, she'd found that the first sense of recall was usually the most detailed. There was really no question on whether or not Gwen was familiar with her attacker. It was getting Gwen to let down her guard enough to say a name without thought.

"Yes." Gwen compressed her lips together, tucking a black strand of that Kendall hair behind her ear. "I recognized him in some manner, but I can't figure out why."

"Someone you went to school with?" Allie didn't want to come across as a heartless bloodhound, but sometimes a more aggressive stance was needed. Gwen had just as much military experience as Allie. Mitch's sister wasn't the type to sit back and allow life to happen around her. She grabbed onto life and scripted it herself...at least, to the best of her ability. "Maybe someone you dated or someone one of your friends dated back in high school?"

Gwen slowly shook her head in disappointment that was clearly aimed at herself.

"Allie, I have gone over and over this practically every minute of the day. I know there's something familiar about my attacker, but it was pitch black. He wore no cologne and smelled of sweat. He was clearly nervous about me fighting back. I was the one to do the talking, and I did it to purposefully aggravate him. I stated that I would shoot him on the count of three, and he wasn't fazed in the least. He did nothing to give himself away, and I couldn't see a single feature without the lights."

"But you *know* his identity," Allie said softly, wondering what else could be said to jog Gwen's memory. "You're just afraid to face the truth of who he is."

CHAPTER NINETEEN

"LANCE, COULD I speak to Dad in private?"

Lance currently had an industrial facemask on, similar to the ones doctors and nurses wore while treating an infectious patient. He'd been using the circular saw to rough cut some stock. Sawdust now coated half of the room where they kept their supply of hardwood for the workshop. His youngest brother pulled the mask up and over his head with a smile.

"Seriously? Why do I always get kicked out of the room when I'm in the middle of a project? You pulled the same crap when we were younger, and I'm beginning to get a complex."

Mitch flashed Lance the bird while he traipsed past his brother to help their dad in the new locker. Gus leaned down to pull a can of lacquer from a storage shelf inside the modern painted locker that Lance had pushed him to install. It was rated to withstand two and a half hours of fire and improved their insurance cost for the shop by half.

Gus had been working on a bedframe in the main shop, putting the finishing touches on it in part of the workshop where they had racks set up under the proper ventilation ducts for drying. It wasn't good to have those fumes hanging around inside the shop all day, or they'd all be loopy by lunchtime.

Lance and their dad worked well together and were doing a number of improvements to modernize the expansive shop to make it safer and more functional. The fact that his dad could tolerate working with Lance eight hours a day was beyond him. Mitch would have strangled him before the second week was out.

"Lance, why don't you go see Brynn for lunch?" Gus asked, though the directive wasn't up for debate. "I'm sure she could use a bit of help for tonight. You know how busy The Cavern gets on Friday nights."

Lance didn't seem to be too irritated that he was being asked to leave his project midstride, and that most likely had to do with Brynn. The two lovebirds couldn't seem to keep their hands off one another. Technically, Mitch was here to see their father for the very same kind of reason.

"Has something happened in the case?" Gus inquired while he walked up the stairs and into the shop. He didn't stop until he'd reached his workbench where he kept a toothpick holder that Gwen had made for him in fourth grade. He plucked a thin wooden stick out of the bunch and stuck it in between his thin lips. "The media coverage regarding Charlene Winston's disappearance is beginning to wane."

"This isn't about the case, Dad."

Gus patted the top of one of the two tall bar-style stools he always kept close to his workbench. They'd been there from the time Mitch was a little boy. They had several worn rows of rungs with rounded seats. He doubted that his father would ever get rid of them.

Mitch remembered having to climb those rungs to perch himself on top of that wooden seat when he explained to his dad why he'd gotten into a fight at school for the first time. There had been a girl in class who he'd liked, and she'd gotten her pigtails pulled by another boy. Mitch had decided that wasn't right, and he was going to fix that boy's wagon.

His response had ended up with him getting into trouble,

but he could still remember the girl's smile as the principal hauled him off the playground. Unfortunately, his quick-thinking reaction had also landed him right here in this hot seat. He didn't get a lecture as much as he'd received a life lesson in the art of being a gentleman.

Quite frankly, Gus was most likely waiting for grandchildren to sit on them so that he could teach them the same lessons he'd taught their parents. Mitch had to grimace another half-smile as he took a seat on the same stool so many years later.

"Ah." Gus nodded as he reached for the old coffee maker that still held the glass carafe with a small crack near the top brown plastic spout. As long as it didn't spring a leak, he'd continue to brew coffee in it every day. "I suspect this is about Allie."

Mitch remained silent for a moment, taking the proffered cup his father slid over to him on the worn smooth wooden surface. He held the warmth of the mug in his hand and wondered why he was even here. Nothing his father said would change the way things with Allie would end.

"This was usually your mother's area of expertise—advice on the female gender." Gus removed his toothpick to take a healthy drink of his coffee, the inside of his mouth evidently immune to the scorching temperature of the rich beverage. It was impossible not to notice the sparkle in his blue eyes. Mitch was taken aback that it wasn't sadness until his father cleared up the misconception. "You know that she's looking down on us right now and giving me the lecture of a lifetime that I don't ruin this moment. I'll tell you one thing—she would have loved Allie's spunk."

"Spunk?" Mitch could use a lot of adjectives to describe Allie, but the word *spunk* hadn't crossed his mind once. With that said, he realized that she had it in spades. He had no doubt that his mother would have adored Allie, but not even Mary Kendall had the power to keep the woman he cared deeply for in Blyth Lake. "Yeah, Allie definitely dances to her own set of tunes."

"And you wish the playlist was yours, as well." Gus set his mug down with a wise smile. "You two have known each other for years. What makes today any different than the rest of them?"

"Allie left the Corps to go to college. She fulfilled her dream of being a profiler with the FBI, which wasn't an easy feat. She's got a lot invested in her career with the Bureau."

Mitch ignored the vibration of his cell phone. Lester Feen had been calling into the station all morning with complaints regarding the edge of his property that bumped up against Raymond Dixon's. The feds still had that section of land cordoned off with tape, and it would likely remain that way for a little while longer in case forensics needed to take another look at the two graves.

"I understand that the two of you took separate paths, but you mentioned Allie's name last year. This relationship that you managed to strike up with her has been going on for quite a while."

"Not really," Mitch admitted, wondering what he was doing at his dad's place to begin with. It didn't escape him that Allie was supposed to leave town in two days, not that the itinerary would be altered if their plan didn't net them the results that they wanted. But he wasn't a young boy needing to be told what to do, and he typically wasn't the type of man to need reassurances. "We spent a weekend together before deciding we made better friends than anything more."

"For who? You or her?"

"For both, I guess."

Gus continued to chew on his toothpick, letting Mitch know that he wasn't fooling him.

"Allie never had a real family, Dad. She didn't have what we have here, and I'm not sure she wants that to change." Mitch recalled Allie saying that the closest thing she had to a family was a pigeon who visited her balcony from time to time. It made him want to embrace her and tell her what he could provide for her. "I did bring up the subject the other day."

"And?"

"Let's just say that it probably wasn't the best time to talk about a relationship." Mitch didn't want his father finding out the truth about the investigation, so he needed to tread carefully here. "Allie originally came here because I called in a favor, but the days and nights we've spent together…I'm not sure I want her to leave for the city. Two weeks isn't enough."

"Tell that to your brothers and sister," Gus said with a rich laugh and a slap of his knee. "Son, time isn't a measure of quantity. And is there a reason the two of you can't continue and see where this thing leads with her in D.C.?"

"A long-distance relationship isn't what I had in mind." Hell, Mitch hadn't had any type of commitment on his brain when he'd returned home. "They never last, anyway."

"You're being awfully general with that assumption," Gus chastised as he reached for a rag to wipe off a dab of stain that had gotten onto the back of his weathered hand. "Distance means nothing if two people belong together."

"Allie worked her ass off to get where she is in her career. I doubt that she'd want to give all that up." Mitch tried to look at the situation from her perspective. No wonder it never crossed her mind to make things between them more permanent. "I don't blame her, either. Everything she has ever strived for is in D.C."

"Everything? Is that right?" Gus raised an eyebrow over the rim of his coffee cup. "Your mother's death taught me that everything material wasn't worth a plug nickel. It was all a meaningless diversion, and family was everything. That woman had more common sense in her pinky than I have in my whole body, so I'd have to go with her on this one."

Mitch understood where his father was coming from, but the hard facts of life weren't so cut and dry. Allie's entire existence was in D.C., and it wasn't fair of Mitch to expect her to give it up based on two weeks and a long-ago, passion-filled weekend.

He'd come here for a sounding board. His dad had given him that and more. His and Allie's friendship spanned over sixteen years. It wasn't likely to end, and considering the sensual nights they'd been spending together…whatever their relationship was morphing into wouldn't disintegrate because of the miles between them.

Mitch didn't know what the hell he was going to do, but being able to come talk to his father told him one thing—he couldn't give up his family for the city.

He wanted it all.

Then again, didn't everyone?

He'd never considered himself a selfish prick before, but he'd never been put in this situation, either.

"I appreciate you listening to me, Dad." Mitch set down the mug, not having the stomach for his dad's battery acid this afternoon. He was hoping to meet Allie for lunch, anyway. "I'll see you at The Cavern later tonight."

Mitch made it to the stairs before his father stopped him.

"Son?"

He turned to find that Gus had taken out his toothpick and was pointing the wooden stick his way.

"Don't let her get away if she's the right one."

Mitch nodded slowly before walking down the woodshed's staircase that led to the entrance. The cold air immediately seeped through his jeans as he exited the large storage shed, which told him it was time to take his vintage leather flight jacket out from the front closet at home.

A home where he would have to walk through the front door alone after Allie headed back to D.C.

He wasn't enough of a selfish prick to stop her from being happy, though.

CHAPTER TWENTY

"**A**LLIE, WE WERE supposed to have left twenty minutes ago."

She was well aware of that, but she was currently staring at the white board in Mitch's living room that she'd been working on practically all weekend. The answer was right in front of her, and she still couldn't connect the dots. It was like a simple arithmetic problem where a decimal had been misplaced by one digit either way.

It was frustrating as hell.

"Five more minutes," Allie said distractedly, looking down at the list of names Brynn had given her yesterday. Two of the men could immediately be crossed out—one had died in a ski accident and the other had been in the hospital with appendicitis at the time of Emma's abduction. "There were quite a lot of people who weren't at that bonfire."

"Deputy Foster being one of them," Mitch pointed out, picking up the black whiteboard marker and crossing one of his employee's names off the list. "Kyle was in the city that night, and he gave a timetable to Thorne that would have made it impossible for him to have been back in the city to abduct Emma."

"The list is getting smaller," Allie murmured, a shot of adrenaline rushing through her. It was abruptly stopped when she thought back over this weekend. They had put such a well thought out, promising plan in place that had gone absolutely nowhere. "Why didn't the unsub make a move on me? We had everything in place, even the disagreement between us that we orchestrated Saturday night at The Cavern."

"Who wasn't at The Cavern Saturday who is on that list?"

"No one," Allie said with frustration, slamming down the sheet of paper on the numerous other files she'd been poring over most of the morning. A glance out the living room window showed her that the rain had yet to let up. "So, that detail should have tipped the scales in our favor. The unsub shouldn't have been able to stop himself from *saving* me. What are we missing, Ken?"

"You're going to be missing a few strands of hair if you call me Ken one more time," Mitch jested, taking Allie by the hand and all but pulling her to her feet. He prevented her witty rebuttal by claiming her lips. She tasted of hot chocolate and mint from the homemade concoction he'd made her for breakfast. He took his time savoring her flavor before pulling away. He shot a quick glance at the white board. "This will all be here when we get back."

He didn't fool her. Even she could hear the frustration lacing his rich tone.

Having a Kendall family dinner while Charlene Winston was still missing was a double-edged sword. Why hadn't the unsub made his move? Had her profile been so far off that she'd led Jay's team on a wild goose chase?

"Fine," Allie muttered, lifting herself up with her knee-high boots and bringing him closer to her. He wrapped his arms around her waist and buried his face in her neck, instantly causing her to smile. "You keep doing that, and I'm sure you can talk me into a few other things, too."

"Would that include a couple of plane tickets in our future?"

Allie couldn't stop her heart from racing at his suggestion. True to his word, he hadn't brought up their relationship since the night they both agreed to table the conversation. What had changed?

"Mitch, we said—"

"We said that we wouldn't discuss us, and I'm not even entering that arena right now." Mitch slowly pulled away until he was able to cradle her face in the palms of his hands. "I'd like to know we have a tentatively scheduled match in the ring, though."

"A long-distance relationship wouldn't be—"

Mitch gently rested his thumb over her lips to stop her from going any further. He wasn't giving her a chance to voice her concerns, but then again, she'd been the one who'd put a lid on this topic of discussion.

"All I'm saying is that maybe it's time you allow something other than a pigeon to visit your apartment now and again."

It took Allie a moment to register that he'd heard every word she'd said two weeks ago about the status of her love life. She cautiously pressed her palms to his chest and allowed the rhythm of her heartbeat to sync with his. Did he believe it was easy for her to spend an entire day with his family as they laughed and shared memories of a joyful childhood? As fond as she was of that pigeon, her Sundays weren't spent in the same manner.

A long-distance relationship would mean that Mitch would have to give those family dinners up at least two weekends a month. Having witnessed his interactions with his family, friends, and neighbors...well, she wasn't so sure he wouldn't come to resent his time with her in D.C.

"Allie?" Mitch caressed her lower lip with his thumb and waited to speak until she'd met his reassuring gaze. "It's just a thought."

"I think I liked it better when we were on the same page," Allie murmured after having cleared her throat twice. She backed up a step to give each of them a little breathing room before he could argue her point. Maybe it was time to head to the family homestead. "Let me grab the meat and cheese tray from the refrigerator. We can't have you forgetting to bring one of the sides again. Gwen would kill you."

Allie was grateful when Mitch didn't stop her from walking out of the living room and into the kitchen. He'd sliced three different block cheeses while she'd rolled the sliced meats, spreading out rows upon rows on a platter. Each sibling brought something to share with the meal, and it was Mitch's turn to bring an appetizer. They had two different boxes of crackers. Ritz and Townhouse were what the small grocery store in town stocked on their shelves.

Their barbequing days were over, and Gus was making a pot roast with homemade mashed potatoes and cooked carrots. She hadn't had a home cooked meal like that since she'd gone to a colleague's housewarming party last year.

"Mitch, should we—" Allie sensed something was wrong the second she walked back into the living room. Mitch was staring down at the list she'd continually agonized over since receiving it from Brynn. It was easy to see he'd made a connection that the rest of them hadn't. She quickly set the appetizer platter on top of the other files. "What is it?"

Mitch shook his head in disbelief before walking over to the white board she'd spent all weekend creating, similar to the one Jay had put together at the police station. He slowly pointed to a name that she'd contemplated herself numerous times. Unfortunately, the implications of it would devastate his family.

"We need something more concrete than the fact that he fits the profile," Allie suggested softly, thinking of the ramifications this would cause to those he loved. What had Mitch remembered that would cause him to zero in on that particular name? "Let's call Jay and have him meet us here to go over the details of what we have. We don't know anything for sure at this point."

"It would make sense." Mitch ran a hand over his face in incredulity, most likely in an attempt to come to terms with whatever dots he'd connected in the short time she'd been in the kitchen. "You once told me this wasn't the type of case where the residents would say they didn't have a clue, but instead that they would recognize the signs that have been there all along. You were right, Allie. If only I'd accepted what was right there in front of us the entire time…"

"We don't know anything for certain at this point, which is why we need to call Jay in on this before we spend dinner with your family."

"Can you imagine how that's going to go?" Mitch stepped back, almost as if he didn't want any part of what the future held once the suspect was brought in for questioning. "How am I going to tell Gwen that Chad's brother—Wesley Schaeffer— attempted to kidnap and kill her all because he wanted a makeshift family that his father and brothers weren't good enough to fill?"

CHAPTER TWENTY-ONE

"T HAT WAS A waste of time," Mitch complained, making a left-hand turn onto First Street.

"No, it wasn't." Allie had been silent ever since Thorne had left the house. "Jay pointed out a couple of wrinkles in your theory, but he was right not to bring Wesley in for questioning right now. If there's a chance that Charlene Winston is still alive, we'd blow any chance of locating her if we show our hand too early."

Wesley Schaeffer.

He hardly seemed like the type of man who could abduct and murder more than eighteen young women over the span of twelve years.

Then again, Mitch couldn't imagine anyone on the numerous lists made over the course of the last five months being responsible for such gruesome murders.

Had Mitch made a miscalculation? Had he just thrown a good man under the bus just to watch its tires rip this man's reputation to shreds?

It wasn't as if Wes had the best standing in the community, but everyone made mistakes or had disagreements. Hadn't Chad's brother done his best to make amends? Truthfully, the Schaeffer family had been through hell and back with Clayton's drunken involvement already.

"We can't bring Wes in for formal questioning based on the

fact that he doesn't have an alibi for the night Emma Irwin went missing," Allie said, tapping her nails on the edge of the tray she'd chosen to set in her lap. "All the other points you made are circumstantial, at best. Plus, Wes lives in Cleveland. That alone makes it difficult to put him at the scenes of the abductions, especially the older ones."

"Think about it," Mitch said, waving to an older gentleman walking his dog. "Wes has been spending more time here ever since Clayton got into legal trouble. He was the only one who would have known, besides Clayton, that Chad was coming home on that particular road at that specific time the night Gwen was attacked."

Gwen's nightmares were what got Mitch thinking about the names on the list. She'd mentioned that it was Chad's face she saw every night in her dreams, and a valid reason her subconscious would switch out the faces were if she'd unconsciously recognized her attacker's resemblance.

Wes fit every other criterion in the profile—he was in his mid-thirties, he came from a broken home, he was a local who knew the personal details of everyone's lives, and he had access to all the victims. All that was left for Thorne to do was connect Wesley Schaeffer to the young girls who weren't from Blyth Lake.

"Everyone in town was aware that Chad and his father were in the city having dinner with Wes and Clayton," Allie pointed out. "And you're neglecting to mention how difficult it would have been to get ahead of Chad and Miles without them recognizing Wes' vehicle, just to turn around and manage to run them off the road."

"It wouldn't have been too difficult if Wes had left the dinner first." Mitch had never thought to ask Chad about the dinner, per se. Neither had Agent Thorne. "We can have all of these questions answered if we brought Wes in for questioning."

"And risk tipping Wes' hand if he truly is our unsub?" Allie shook her head in disagreement as she rested her elbow against the window. "Jay needs to handle the paperwork properly. He's going back to the station now to hopefully get us enough evidence to hold Wesley in custody should this backfire on us. That would at least buy Jay some time in order to get a search warrant for any of the locations where Charlene could be held."

"We should be at the station with him."

Mitch didn't like being told to sit on the sidelines when a big play was about to take place, but Thorne hadn't given them a choice.

"And what if Wesley calls Chad while we're all at dinner? One wrong word and this could blow up in our faces." Allie looked out the window with a frown on her face. "I just don't understand what happened Saturday night. I mean, we carefully orchestrated an argument to force the unsub's hand. If Wesley is our unsub, why wouldn't he have made an attempt to add me to his so-called family? He was right there with the rest of your family, hearing every word we said to one another."

Mitch tightened his grip on the steering wheel as he went over the facts in his head one more time. Small pieces of threads were beginning to be sewn together, but it was as if the sewing machine had stopped with the needle stuck in the fabric.

"Did your dad ask why we were going to be late?"

"Dad didn't answer his cell phone, so I left him a voicemail." Mitch guided his vehicle onto the gravel lane that led to his childhood home. "That was for the best, because he would have asked what was causing the delay. I didn't want to have to evade the question over the phone."

Mitch wasn't surprised to see the number of vehicles in the driveway after they cleared the knot of pine trees that cloaked the property from the road. The clouds from Friday hadn't quite disappeared and there was still a fine mist hanging in the air, leaving a sheen to glisten on the trucks and one lone red Jeep.

Noah and Reese had probably already started a fire in the hearth. Lance was most likely trying to sneak a piece of pie before dinner without Brynn noticing, and Jace was no doubt talking to the rest of the Kendall clan about the mare he was set to acquire at the beginning of the year. As for Chad and Gwen, they were almost certainly going over the details for the Thanksgiving meal that would take place in a couple of weeks and making sure every single menu item was covered. Mitch hated planning the meals. He was much better at eating them.

How could Mitch look Chad in the eye today and feign that the man's life wasn't about to be torn in two?

He shoved the gearshift into park and then turned the key in the ignition, sitting with Allie for a moment as the engine cooled down. She hadn't even reached for her seat belt, which told him that she was having doubts about getting through this evening, as well.

"The unsub is angry at your family, and I didn't see that in Wesley's mannerisms on Saturday night," Allie said with a small shake of her head. Seeing as she'd been working on adjusting her profile this morning, she wore her hair gathered at the base of her neck. "As a matter of fact, he seemed rather content. Almost as if…"

"As if what?"

"I don't know." Allie was clearly frustrated. "I'm missing something."

Maybe Mitch was way off base. Maybe Wesley had nothing to do with this investigation, and the remorse over believing someone was guilty with such close ties to his family would eventually fade. That would certainly solve a lot of issues.

"I want to eat dinner and then head to the station." Mitch grabbed the keys and unfastened his seatbelt. "I don't want to linger when we could be helping Thorne investigate Wes."

Mitch opened the driver's side door and got out of the vehicle, resigning himself to spending the next couple of hours with his family instead of working the investigation. Thorne should at least have most of the groundwork laid, meaning there was still a chance they'd get some answers tonight.

Mitch had just cleared the trunk of the car when he saw the brightest flash of light that he hadn't witnessed since his days in the Corps.

There was no time to move, to protect his face, or most importantly—reach Allie.

The massive explosion originated from one side of the home that Gus and Mary Kendall had worked so hard to build so long ago. The windows shattered, the wood splintered, and the remaining mass of building materials were engulfed in angry orange flames that sought to scorch everything they touched, including those individuals who'd been inside and meant everything to him—his family.

CHAPTER TWENTY-TWO

THE CONTINUOUS RINGING in Allie's ears wouldn't stop, and she blinked several times to try and make out what had happened after Mitch stepped out of the car. She lifted a hand to the right side of her face, only to come away with blood on her fingertips.

"Mitch?"

She could only hear her voice on the inside of her head. It seemed muffled and distant.

Weren't they parked in front of the Kendall's family homestead? Or had they been in an accident and she'd only imagined Mitch pulling the car next to Gwen's Jeep?

Allie shifted in the passenger seat to check on Mitch, but shards of glass covering the meat and cheese platter were scattered all around. She didn't care and reached out for him, anyway.

He wasn't behind the wheel.

Allie immediately shoved the plate onto the floorboard in her attempt to find Mitch, but she abruptly stopped when she saw the...carnage. There was no other way to describe what was left of a home that had stood proudly for decades.

Flames engulfed what was left of the house. Wood, drywall, and most certainly contents of the home were now scattered within a fifty-yard radius, if not more. The ring of debris nearly reached the workshop where Gus and Lance worked through the day. She and Mitch had pulled into the driveway, but it was he who had been standing outside of the vehicle when the explosion had struck.

"Mitch!"

Again, her muffled voice seemed suppressed and to be coming from a source far away.

Allie scrambled out of the damaged vehicle, ignoring the tiny chunks of safety glass that were abrading her hands. She practically spilled out from the mangled door, barely catching herself before landing on one knee. Red and black ashes was now raining down from the sky above as she virtually crawled around the back tire of the car.

Mitch was nowhere to be found.

"Mitch!" Allie yelled, using the back bumper for leverage as she got to her feet. The ringing in her ears was beginning to subside, but just barely. Her heart beat hard against her chest as movement came about eight feet in front of her. Mitch was rolling onto his side as he attempted to stand. "Mitch, don't move. You're bleeding and—"

"Move out of the way."

Allie had never in all her time in the Bureau heard such desperation and pain laced between the words of such a directive. It was clear that Mitch only had one goal, and that was to reach the house.

But there was nothing left but burning pyres, and anything inside had been destroyed right along with it.

She swallowed the sob that had caught in the back of her throat, concentrating solely on the man in front of her. The heat of the blast had given Mitch's face second degree burns, and some of the debris must have made contact with his skin. Blood was dripping down his forehead, diverting around his eyebrow and rolling down the side of his face.

"Mitch, we need to call this in—"

Nothing she said was going to stop Mitch from going inside that inferno, but that wouldn't prevent her from trying to get him to see reason—nothing inside could have survived that explosion. He shook off her grasp as he took off running, calling out for his dad, brothers, and sister.

The anguish in his muffled, guttural screams brought her to tears, but she still ran after him. She didn't stop until she'd managed to get in front of him and grab his shirt.

"Mitch, they're gone." Allie dug her boots into the gravel as Mitch continued to walk forward. He was physically stronger than she was, but she would do everything in her power to prevent him from being hurt worse. She wouldn't lose him like they'd lost... "Stop! Just stop, Mitch. They're gone, and you trying to get in there will only get you killed, too."

His suffering shone bright in those blue eyes of his, telling her that he didn't care what happened to himself at this moment. Allie did, and she wouldn't allow him to take from her what had been stolen from him.

It all made sense now.

The unsub had taken the very thing that the Kendalls had taken from him.

An eye for an eye.

She should have seen this coming.

Mitch had come home to lead the revolt against the evil inhabiting this town. He was the guardian and defender of his family, just as the unsub was to his makeshift gravesite.

An eye for an eye.

"Let go of me, Allie," Mitch directed in such a guttural tone that it tore her heart in two. His grip on her shoulders were tight as he moved her to the side, once again telling her that nothing she said was getting through to him. "They're my family, and they are *not* gone."

Mitch took off once again, getting as close to the flames as possible as he looked for a way into the destruction. He began calling for his dad and siblings one by one, his voice becoming hoarser with each name. Allie was truly afraid he'd somehow find a way to enter the inferno as he edged closer to the flames in hopes of saving his family, thereby taking away the one person who was now *her* only family.

Allie continued to try and pull him away from the red-hot blaze, denying him the chance to die along with the rest of his siblings. She followed him all the way around the porch, spotting the falling piece of wood as they rounded the corner. Using every bit of strength she had left, she rammed Mitch from the back until they were both on the ground.

"Mitch, please stop," Allie cried out desperately as he got to his knees. Tears were running down his cheeks and blending in with the blood and soot. His pain and anguish were almost too much to bear. She managed to get to her knees and take his face into her hands, hoping he would finally focus on her instead of the destruction all around them. "Please."

Her last word came out as a sob, but it was no match for the guttural cry that was torn from his throat. The agonizing scream wasn't natural, and she did the only thing she could—she wrapped her arms around him and held on as tightly as she could.

"I won't leave you, Mitch," Allie whispered over and over again, wanting desperately to erase his pain. She clung to him. "I won't leave you. I promise."

Allie had no idea how long they stayed on their knees. The entire town would have heard the explosion, so help should be arriving any minute. But it wasn't the piercing resonances of sirens from firetrucks or law enforcement that broke through the residual ringing in her ears—it was the miraculous sound of voices coming from the Kendall family.

Mitch and Allie tore themselves apart to find Lance running toward them from the back of the house. Brynn was close behind, followed by Noah, Reese, Jace, Shae, Gwen, and finally Gus. They all but converged on Mitch and Allie as they all embraced.

"How are you—"

"…it was a call from Chad."

"He warned us to get out of the house…"

"…a bomb next to the gas meter and…"

Gus began to move everyone farther into the yard as explanations began to surface one after another. It was clear to Allie that Chad had somehow figured out that his own brother was responsible for the lives of those young girls about the same time she had. Maybe he confronted Wes or maybe Wes had even tried to stop his brother from being at the Kendall's homestead before the bomb went off.

No matter how it had happened, Chad had managed to contact Gwen and alert them to the fact that there was an explosive device somewhere near the house and that everyone needed to get to safety. Allie couldn't imagine the horrible realization Chad had experienced in knowing his own flesh and blood was responsible for so many deaths.

Those sirens she'd been expecting to hear finally broke through the roar of the fire, causing the close group to finally disperse as they all quickly made their way toward the damaged vehicles. There would be time to cherish their immense relief once the man responsible was brought in to answer for his crimes.

"I don't see Jay's car. Let me grab my cell phone out of my purse." Allie separated herself from what would be an all too brief reunion. Mitch still had a tight grip on her hand, but he was nodding his agreement. The danger to this family and to the residents of Blyth Lake wasn't over, and Chad's life might very well hang in the balance. There was no way that Wesley would have allowed him to make that call without trying to stop his brother. "I'll speak with Jay, and then we can—"

The SUV that Mitch had assigned to Byron quickly passed the firetrucks and came to an abrupt halt within ten feet from where they were standing. The window was already rolled down to deliver a message that no one was quite ready for—especially Gwen.

"Wesley Schaeffer has taken his dad and brothers hostage up at the lake," Byron called out, waving for Mitch to get into the SUV. The deputy's kind gaze landed on Gwen. "I'm sorry, but Wesley is holding them all prisoner at the end of one of the piers."

CHAPTER TWENTY-THREE

"I 'M GLAD TO hear that you and your family are okay, Sheriff."

Mitch ignored the burning sensation in both eyes, as well as the all-consuming fire that had been set to his face. He would have endured the suffering from the depths of hell if it meant that his family was safe and sound. There were no words to describe the relief he'd experienced upon hearing the voices of his loved ones.

And that included Allie.

"Agent Thorne is already on the scene, and he's called in a negotiator." Byron's tone indicated that the additional help wouldn't be necessary. He took one of the turns heading up to the lake a little too wide, but he easily managed to get the SUV back under control. "At least the media hasn't gotten wind of the situation yet."

That's because every damn reporter that had been waiting for a break in the case was covering the explosion at his childhood home that no longer existed. As if Allie had read his mind, her hand came out of nowhere to rest on his shoulder. She'd refused to stay at the house and had gotten into the back seat of the vehicle before Bryon had peeled out of the driveway.

Gwen and the rest of the family were no doubt seconds behind them.

Allie had done all she could to prevent him from going into

the raging fire, and she'd been right to do so. He hadn't been thinking clearly. In all honesty, he wasn't now.

"Wesley Schaeffer has nothing left to lose," Allie said cautiously, her bloody hand slipping from his shirt. She was bleeding in various places, just like him. Technically, they both needed to be looked over at the hospital, but there hadn't been time. He squeezed his eyes tight, but not against the burning sensation. His chest cavity was like a vise around his heart and lungs. It was damn hard to breathe as the aftermath settled around them. "He's ready to die, and take what little of his family he has left with him."

"I can't wrap my head around the fact that Wesley killed all those girls," Byron said, finally making the last turn that would take them to the main pier at the marina. He'd been given the right location by Thorne, who'd called to ensure that the Kendall family had made it out of the inferno alive. "I mean, Wesley Schaeffer. It's unbelievable."

The lingering mist appeared to have morphed into a fog that went on for miles. The weather conditions certainly wouldn't make this upcoming negotiation any easier. Mitch hated to admit that he doubted any conversation would take place, especially considering the fact that Wes hadn't succeeded in what he'd set out to do—rob Mitch of his family.

Hell, maybe Wes had been hoping to take Mitch's life, as well.

"How did Thorne know that Wes brought his father and brothers up to the lake?" Mitch asked, still trying to connect the pieces of today's timeline.

"Rose was the one who called in to tell us that something was wrong with Chad. I mean, the phone literally rang the moment we heard the explosion."

Mitch assumed that meant Wes had thought he'd been successful in taking out the Kendalls. It was by happenstance that Mitch and Allie had been delayed, but that small fact would have likely given Wes extreme pleasure in knowing that Mitch had been left behind without his family.

What had Allie muttered when they'd gotten into the SUV?

An eye for an eye.

"Apparently, Chad was limping and bleeding as he got out of Wes' truck. Rose said she immediately went over to see what was wrong when Wes waved a gun in her direction, telling her to stay away from them."

A firearm wasn't in Wes' toolbox, but the man had clearly accepted his fate. It didn't matter what weapon he used now, as long as he was able to take his father and brothers with him.

"This is the end, Mitch," Allie murmured as she opened the back door after Byron had brought the vehicle to a stop, alongside numerous other vehicles. Three of the unmarked cars belonged to the FBI. "The best we can hope for is that Thorne called in a SWAT team, and that the sniper has a clear headshot. Otherwise, we're about to lose three more innocent victims."

One of those targets being Chad Schaeffer. He was family, as far as Mitch was concerned. The man had somehow been able to warn Gwen that there was an explosive near the homestead, allowing Mitch's father and siblings to make it to safety. Regardless, his sister loved Chad.

Mitch would do everything in his power to see to it that his sister's happiness remained intact—even if that meant sacrificing himself. He moved to the back of the SUV and dropped the tailgate. He reached in and removed a Remington 700 with a large scope attached. He checked the breach and chambered a .308 round from the magazine well.

If Wesley Schaeffer wanted to exact some type of revenge, then Mitch would see to it that hostages were traded to appease the darkness inside of that madman.

"Allie, I'm going to need your help with Thorne."

She remained quiet as they all left the vehicle and slowly made their way to where Thorne stood with just two other agents. He must have called them in right after leaving Mitch's house before diverting them up here to this so-called standoff. It wasn't much of one, considering Wes held all the cards…for now.

"Allie has something to discuss with you," Mitch called out, interrupting whatever Thorne was saying to the other agents while trying not to appear rushed.

"Mitch, you—"

Mitch turned quickly so that only Allie could hear the desperation in his voice.

"You already said that this was the end," Mitch whispered, taking a hold of her arm as he leaned down to speak into her ear. "Waiting is only going to result in four deaths, and you know it."

Allie's gaze flickered down the pier and through the fog, the four men barely visible. Even she had to see the urgency in this matter. Yes, Thorne had to follow procedure. But Mitch was still the goddamned sheriff of this town and those were his people about to meet their maker.

"I made you a promise," Allie murmured, catching Mitch off guard. Those green flecks that he'd come to love so much were subdued with worry and fear. "Ten minutes ago, I made a vow not to leave you. Can you do the same for me, Mitch?"

The last half an hour had honestly blurred together, but she'd grabbed his attention now. And she'd purposefully used his given name that captured his attention every time she used it. Of course, he'd heard her oath that she'd promised to him under duress. He just wasn't sure he could keep a promise with what waited for him at the end of that row of wooden planks.

"I can't leave you alone with a pigeon, now can I?" Mitch asked softly, all but telling her that he'd do everything in his power to make it back to her.

Allie stared at him intently for a few more seconds before making her decision. He breathed a sigh of relief when she stepped around him, calling out to Thorne and the others. She began to explain what happened at his father's place and managed to divert their attention long enough to give Mitch a head start down the dock after passing the Remington off to his deputy and unbuttoning the latch of his holster. If he needed to draw quickly, he didn't want to waste the second it would take in the delay of his action.

Mitch jogged quickly with his hands in the air and had made it halfway down the pier before he heard Thorne calling out his name in anger.

Well, he could get in line.

Wesley Schaeffer's soulless eyes were directed right at Mitch, watching his every move. The heavy fog seemed to embrace him in an ominous world that had been prepared by the evil he commanded.

"Is Gwen..." Chad was leaning against one of the pilings of the pier, looking more in need of a hospital than Mitch or Allie. The gunshot wound to his leg was evident even with the dark blue handkerchief tied around it. There was also a knot on his temple that was leaking blood.

"Gwen is fine," Mitch said, maintaining an even tone as he managed to keep his hands in the air. He needed to appear as nonthreatening as possible, given the circumstances. It was a wonder Wes hadn't already taken out the Schaeffer men. "The entire family made it out just before the explosion."

Mitch had to hold himself back as fury morphed Wes' features into something unrecognizable. He swung the firearm until it was aimed directly at Chad, who humbly didn't even flinch. The man had probably gone numb inside after discovering that his brother was a fucking monster.

Miles stepped up to the plate though, and immediately put himself in between Wes and Chad.

"Wesley James, please don't do this," Miles pleaded, holding his weathered hands out in front of him. "Please. I'm begging you."

The middle name thing wasn't going to work, but Miles appeared desperate. Who wouldn't be in this situation? Clayton was standing next to Chad with a look of shock across his features.

No one—especially not the Schaeffers—would ever get over the fact that one of their own blood relatives had done something so horrific to the good people of this town.

"You took away my family."

Mitch had never taken his gaze off of Wesley. It was clear that Wes was talking to him, and any dialogue at this point was helpful.

"Wes, we can get you the help you need." Mitch somehow managed to get the words out even though the only thing he wanted to do was put a slug in the middle of this fucker's forehead. Gone were the regrets that someone he'd known his entire life had kept something so foul hidden from his loved ones. It was time to bring this to an end. "Put down the weapon. You don't want to hurt your father or brothers."

"You took my family," Wesley cried out, on the verge of weeping. "They were mine. I took care of them all these years when no one else could be bothered."

Allie had been right in that Wes was angry with the Kendalls. Noah's homecoming had been the beginning of Wes' downfall. Lance returning home to find the pictures of Wes' numerous victims who he'd hidden away had only added to his plight. Jace and Shae's role in uncovering the underwater gravesite was the final straw, but it hadn't ended there.

Unbeknownst to all of them, Gwen Kendall had taken Wes' brother...a part of his family that had been his own flesh and blood.

"I can take you to them." Mitch began to lower his hands while hoping to be able to draw his firearm from its holster, aim, and fire faster than Wes could decide to pull his trigger. "I can have Agent Thorne exhume their bodies and have them brought back to the morgue."

"You won't do that. I'm not an idiot." Wes wiped away his tears with the back of his hand. It gave Mitch the opportunity to lower his hands to his sides. It appeared that an eye for an eye was about to come to fruition. "And I can't leave this world without my family."

Wesley pointed the pistol at his father, causing Miles to quickly step back. Chad rested a hand on his father's back in reassurance. As for Clayton, well, he appeared ready to jump in the water...which wasn't such a bad idea.

"Wesley, you can see that this is a no win situation, right?" Allie's sweet but determined voice came out of nowhere, right before she exited the fog to come stand by Mitch's side. "You might get off one shot before Mitch puts one in you. You'll only be taking your father, leaving behind your brothers to fend for themselves. Isn't that what you've been fighting to save? Family?"

"We'd be with Mom," Wes whispered, as if he were convincing himself that he could make this work. "We'd be a family again."

"No," Allie said sadly with a shake of her head. "No, because you can't take all three of them with you."

Mitch witnessed Wes' index finger become white as he applied pressure to the trigger.

"Wesley, there's a way for all of you to remain together," Allie suggested with more kindness than Mitch could have done in this instance. "Your family loves you unconditionally. No matter what happens, your father and brothers will be by your side."

"But I won't have *them* with me," Wes exclaimed as he gestured toward the lake that no longer held his victims.

"Those young girls were never yours to take, Wesley." Allie continually said Wes' name over and over again, keeping him engaged long enough so that Mitch could palm his weapon. He didn't believe for one moment that Wes wasn't aware of his surroundings, but the time had come to put an end to the darkness that had plagued Blyth Lake for far too long. "I don't have a family, and it would be nice to have someone to talk to about my fears. But who would I do that with if you're no longer here?"

Mitch bit off the string of curse words that flew through his mind when Allie stepped forward, blocking his ability to get a shot off and finish what Wesley had started over twelve years ago. Mitch shifted his footing so that he would be able to grab Allie by her jacket and yank her backward when the moment came for him to shoot and kill.

She took another step closer to Wesley, causing her to be out of reach.

Damn it.

He'd almost lost his family today. That now included Allie, and he wasn't going to lose her. Unfortunately, he could only observe in astonishment as she did what no one would have been able to do given the circumstances—she apprehended the Blyth Lake Serial Killer without further bloodshed.

"Wesley, I don't want to be left alone," Allie said softly.

She was now standing directly in front of his weapon. She slowly reached out with a steady hand and laid her fingers over his. Mitch couldn't breathe until the firearm was released into her possession. As a matter of fact, he was pretty damn sure bile hit the back of his throat.

Thorne came out of nowhere, successfully apprehending Wes while Allie continued to assure him that he wouldn't be alone. The man was now openly weeping, pleading with his father and brothers. He continued to scream that he loved them and had only tried to save those young girls from a life of loneliness.

It was honestly so pitiful that someone who had caused such heartache could be so broken. Even Miles appeared torn, and Allie continued to explain to the older man why it was so important that he stand by Wes' side in the aftermath of this tragedy.

For one, Charlene Winston was still missing.

Two, there was a lot of information they still needed to gather that spanned all the years of Wes' crimes. They'd only touched on the surface, and this was a way to give grieving families peace from the unknown.

"Excuse me."

Billy Stanton was trying to get through to Chad, who continued to ask Allie about Gwen. He didn't have to wait for an answer. Gwen came running past Billy to reach Chad. She didn't even look twice when she passed Thorne escorting Wes down the pier to a waiting unmarked vehicle.

"Chad, let's get you on the ground so that we can see what we're dealing with," Billy instructed, motioning for his partner to aid in the transition of their patient. "Gwen, please give us some space. You can ride with Chad to the hospital."

Mitch finally holstered his weapon, taking in his environment…all the while keeping a close eye on Allie. She might have had a steady hand when she'd taken Wes' firearm, but he could see the slight tremor in her fingers as she brushed aside the thick strand that liked to frame her face.

"You need a paramedic," Allie said, taking Mitch's hand to lead him down the pier. He shook his head, really just needing a moment to himself. "Mitch, you—"

"One minute." Mitch didn't give Allie the ability to argue. He walked over to the other side of the pier and lowered himself until he was using the round wooden piling about the size of a telephone pole as a seat. "Come here."

Mitch drew her to him, resting his forehead against her stomach. She gently placed her hands on the back of his head, giving him the privacy he needed to come to terms with what had happened here today.

Allie had always had his six before when he needed her, and now was no different. He could hear his name being called in the distance, most likely looking for guidance on how to handle the questions the locals would undoubtedly want to hear from him and not from an outsider.

He honestly wasn't sure what he'd say.

Reputations had been tarnished due to many undeserved seeds of doubt.

A good family had been destroyed and another had lost their ancestral home.

A town had suffered the loss of too many of their loved ones.

"There is a lot of healing to be done here," Allie whispered, kneeling so that he could see her beautiful face. The small cuts to her cheeks had stopped bleeding, but the scars would no doubt remain. "They're going to need you to lead the way, Mitch

Kendall. You are their protector. Their leader in times of trouble."

It would take a lifetime to mend the wounds that had been inflicted on the residents of Blyth Lake by one of their own children.

Was Mitch the one to lead that effort?

Yes, he could be.

He might have initially fought taking on the title of sheriff, but Blyth Lake was his town. He wouldn't let this heartbreak tear down everything this place stood for, and he sure as hell didn't want to do it alone.

"I think Blyth Lake needs a mascot."

"I'm sorry?" Allie asked, clearly lost by the direction Mitch had taken their conversation. She rested her knees against the wet wood, searching his eyes in what was probably fear that his wounds were worse than she'd first thought. "Mitch, what are you…"

"Your pigeon, Allie," Mitch replied with a small smile as recognition finally had those green flecks in her eyes sparkling with relief. "Remember, we can't leave family behind. Do you think we can catch him?"

CHAPTER TWENTY-FOUR

One year and one month later…

"THAT'S TOO BIG," Jace complained, holding the saw against his leg and refusing to walk toward the eight-foot pine tree. "There's no way that will fit inside the new house."

Jace was right, but Mitch would let his brothers argue that point if it meant he got to stand back and not become involved in the chaos that was the annual hunt for the family Christmas tree.

They had all opted to come to a Christmas tree farm rather than using a small lot with slim pickings. Every one of them had bundled up in winter clothing, along with the appropriate tools. Hats, scarves, and gloves had been collected, and now the search was on.

Unfortunately, they were running out of daylight hours and dusk would be falling soon. Mitch would give them another twenty minutes to choose before he began cutting down the pine tree he'd had eye on for the past forty-five minutes.

"You always were more of an observer when it came to your brothers and sister," Gus said, holding a thermos of coffee that would hopefully see him through this ordeal. Mitch might be asking for some if this latest mission took longer than an hour. And if last year was anything to go by, picking out a Christmas tree was akin to planning a wedding. "Never liked to get involved, and somehow always managed to smooth things over in the end."

"Nah," Mitch denied, his gaze swinging over to his where his sister stood with her gloved hands resting on her hips. The baby bump was slightly noticeable and endearing to see. Chad was by her side, but he wasn't quite the same man he had been thirteen months ago. Hell, who would be after finding out his own flesh and blood had been capable of something so brutal? "Gwen's taken over that role with ease. Look at how good she's been for the Schaeffers."

Gwen had stood by Chad through thick and thin ever since Wes' arrest—the long, drawn out trial, the mixed and torn reactions from longtime friends and neighbors, and her own emotions when it came to reconciling her pregnancy in the midst of all that turmoil.

Mitch still believed that the significance of new life was a turning point for Chad and Gwen. They'd needed a miracle, and he firmly believed that their mother was running the show from up above.

As for Charlene Winston, she'd been found safe and sound in one of the empty renovated cottages. Last Mitch had heard, Charlene was a number one *New York Times* bestselling author with the recount of her harrowing experience.

"This one will fit if we bend the tip a smidgen," Lance argued, taking a step back and eyeing the Christmas tree he refused to leave behind. It had been ten minutes since he first laid eyes on the oversized pine. "Brynn, what about this one for The Cavern?"

"Wait just a second," Gwen said, adjusting her earmuffs as she shot their younger brother a look of annoyance. "I think that one would look great in my office."

"I take it back." Mitch couldn't help but smile at the way Lance got under Gwen's skin. "Gwen is the peacekeeper unless it comes to Lance."

Gus laughed and began to unscrew the lid to his thermos. Even he believed they were going to be here for at least another hour.

"Since when are we decorating the office?" Chad wrapped an arm around her waist, his hand laying protectively over the baby. "I thought Beth Ann already hung some garland on the wooden railing."

"Yeah, but it's not enough."

"Gwen, you're not getting my tree for the office," Lance complained, looking around for Brynn to back him up. He was going to be disappointed, because Mitch had seen Tiny, Harlan, and Chester all but shoving a huge pine tree through the front door of the bar last night. "Blondie?"

"Tiny already got a tree for The Cavern, and he set it up last night," Brynn informed Lance, coming around the other side of the pine tree. Her blonde ponytail bounced as she tried to compromise with her fiancé. "But I'll let you get this Charlie Brown tree over here to put near the dart board."

"What time is Allie due in next week?" Gus asked, raising the lid to the thermos that had been transformed into a steaming cup of coffee. "Was she able to get her last case wrapped up?"

"Allie was hoping to have her desk cleaned out by Wednesday. She couldn't tell me much about the investigation she was working on, but I do know they made an arrest yesterday. All that's left is some paperwork."

True to Allie's word, she hadn't left him.

She'd taken the rest of her vacation days after Wes' arrest, prolonging her time here in Blyth Lake. They'd gotten on a rotation schedule with who spent what weekend where. It had been a hard adjustment, but so worth it.

Allie had returned to D.C. and immediately put in a request

to transfer to the FBI's field office in Cleveland. It had taken a very long time, but the approval had been given last month. Beginning in January, Allie would officially be a Blyth Lake resident for good.

"What about this one?" Shae called out, her nose red from the dropping temperatures. She used her mitten to point toward a seven-foot tree. "It's bushy."

"And smaller," Jace exclaimed, holding up his saw in victory. He even called out a battle cry that sounded more like a wounded animal than a warrior. "Are we all in agreement?"

"Wait a second," Allie called out, causing everyone to turn around at the sound of that sweet voice he'd been missing for over a week. Phone calls didn't count. "Don't I get a say in the matter?"

"Son of a gun," Mitch muttered, walking quickly toward her to scoop her up in his arms. Her light laugh echoed throughout the trees. "Damn, I've missed you."

Mitch buried his face in her scarf, wishing more than anything it was her bare neck and that they were back home in front of the fireplace where he could take his time loving her.

"I've missed you, Ken," Allie whispered, knowing that would make him want to get her home even faster. She waited until he'd set her down on the soft blanket of snow before tilting her heart-shaped face for a kiss. "You can put in a request to change the population sign. As of today, I'm officially a resident."

The others had heard her declaration. Hoots and hollers made their way through the family, but Mitch quickly managed to divert their attention back to the task at hand. He didn't want to take any longer than necessary, and he made a mental note to tag the perfect tree for their living room. He and Allie could come back tomorrow to create their own tradition.

"You might be a federal agent, but there is no way in hell you could have tracked us out in the middle of a Christmas tree farm without the aid of technology." Mitch raised an eyebrow with suspicion. "Did you trace my cell phone?"

"Why would I need to do that when I have your dad?" Allie lifted up on her tiptoes to plant a kiss on his cheek. "Didn't you know? He's one of my confidential informants. I called dibs, so you can't have him."

Allie laughed as she walked away to join the others around the seven-foot-tall Christmas tree that would go into the newly-built Kendall family home. Granted, it wasn't the same house that Mary Kendall had raised her children in, but it was a smaller version that their father could maintain on his own.

The home had a second bedroom for a guest and an office for his personal business, but the largest room in the house was the kitchen with an adjoining dining room. The Kendall Sunday dinners would need plenty of room in the very near future. Gus used the rest of the insurance money to put an upgrade on the workshop, much to Lance's delight.

"Thanks, Dad." Mitch crossed his arms and settled in to watch his family as they got to enjoy another Christmas. Times like these shouldn't be taken for granted. "It just wasn't the same without her."

Gus nodded his acknowledgement and refilled the lid to the thermos. He quietly handed it over, and Mitch was relatively sure that the weather had nothing to do with the sheen in the father's eyes. It wasn't hard to come to the conclusion that Mitch's sentiment had been given a different meaning in his father's reflection.

No, these special moments weren't the same without Mary Kendall.

"This was all your mother ever wanted," Gus said after clearing his throat. He smiled with fatherly love, nodding his approval as laughter and conversation ensued from his children and their significant others. "Mary dreamed of having you kids raise your families here. I miss her more every day, but I'll be here to enjoy every second of this and report back to her when my time comes. That woman will always be my heart and soul."

And after all...*home is where the heart is.*

~ The End ~

It's always bittersweet to say goodbye to a series, but each of the Kendall siblings received their HEA (Happily Ever After). I adored these heroes and heroines, this town, and the secondary characters...so thank you for following their journeys.

I've recently switched creative gears and released a cozy paranormal mystery series! I would love for you to give this magical world a try. Trust me, you'll be wishing these unique and comical characters could spring to life with a twitch of your nose!

www.kennedylayne.com/magical-blend.html

Magical Blend

An inherited tea shop, a quaint little Connecticut town, and its quirky residents have Raven Marigold believing her luck is about to change for the better. Of course, that was before she and her best friend found a dead body in the back of the charming store. Things go from bad to worse when Raven begins to hear a talking cat spouting on and on about magic and mayhem.

Once Raven accepts that she's not losing her mind, she finds herself in the middle of a murder investigation while discovering her family's unusual lineage—the Marigolds are bona fide witches!

'Tis the season to be scared and delighted…this wickedly charming tale includes magical tea blends, an enchanting spell book, and an eerie cottage on the edge of town that contains a special surprise you won't want to miss!

Books by Kennedy Layne

Paramour Bay Mysteries
Magical Blend
Bewitching Blend
Enchanting Blend

Office Roulette Series
Means (Office Roulette, Book One)
Motive (Office Roulette, Book Two)
Opportunity (Office Roulette, Book Three)

Keys to Love Series
Unlocking Fear (Keys to Love, Book One)
Unlocking Secrets (Keys to Love, Book Two)
Unlocking Lies (Keys to Love, Book Three)
Unlocking Shadows (Keys to Love, Book Four)
Unlocking Darkness (Keys to Love, Book Five)

Surviving Ashes Series
Essential Beginnings (Surviving Ashes, Book One)
Hidden Ashes (Surviving Ashes, Book Two)
Buried Flames (Surviving Ashes, Book Three)
Endless Flames (Surviving Ashes, Book Four)
Rising Flames (Surviving Ashes, Book Five)

CSA Case Files Series

Captured Innocence (CSA Case Files 1)

Sinful Resurrection (CSA Case Files 2)

Renewed Faith (CSA Case Files 3)

Campaign of Desire (CSA Case Files 4)

Internal Temptation (CSA Case Files 5)

Radiant Surrender (CSA Case Files 6)

Redeem My Heart (CSA Case Files 7)

A Mission of Love (CSA Case Files 8)

Red Starr Series

Starr's Awakening(Red Starr, Book One)

Hearths of Fire (Red Starr, Book Two)

Targets Entangled (Red Starr, Book Three)

Igniting Passion (Red Starr, Book Four)

Untold Devotion (Red Starr, Book Five)

Fulfilling Promises (Red Starr, Book Six)

Fated Identity (Red Starr, Book Seven)

Red's Salvation (Red Starr, Book Eight)

The Safeguard Series

Brutal Obsession (The Safeguard Series, Book One)

Faithful Addiction (The Safeguard Series, Book Two)

Distant Illusions (The Safeguard Series, Book Three)

Casual Impressions (The Safeguard Series, Book Four)

Honest Intentions (The Safeguard Series, Book Five)

Deadly Premonitions (The Safeguard Series, Book Six)

About the Author

First and foremost, I love life. I love that I'm a wife, mother, daughter, sister… and a writer.

I am one of the lucky women in this world who gets to do what makes them happy. As long as I have a cup of coffee (maybe two or three) and my laptop, the stories evolve themselves and I try to do them justice. I draw my inspiration from a retired Marine Master Sergeant that swept me off of my feet and has drawn me into a world that fulfills all of my deepest and darkest desires. Erotic romance, military men, intrigue, with a little bit of kinky chili pepper (his recipe), fill my head and there is nothing more satisfying than making the hero and heroine fulfill their destinies.

Thank you for having joined me on their journeys…

Email: kennedylayneauthor@gmail.com

Facebook: facebook.com/kennedy.layne.94

Twitter: twitter.com/KennedyL_Author

Website: www.kennedylayne.com

Newsletter: www.kennedylayne.com/newslettertext.html